THE SPIDER:
BUILDERS OF THE DARK EMPIRE

MASTER OF MEN!

BUILDERS OF THE DARK EMPIRE

By Grant Stockbridge

ALTUS PRESS • 2019

CHAPTER 1
LOOT OF THE SEA

NIGHT AND low-scudding cloudrack smothered down upon the heaving Atlantic, upon the rusty old freighter *Remodo*. Braced straddled-legged in her bows stood Richard Wentworth. He was wet with spray and beneath his feet he felt the surge and lunge as the steamer battled rising seas. But it was something other than fear for the vessel's safety that pulled him alertly up on his toes, that tightened the fighting muscles of his shoulders.

Through the creak and groan of tackle, through the slobbering slap of waves against the prow, his keen-attuned ears caught the furtive footfalls of a man behind him. The killer he had expected was creeping forward to murder him!

Richard Wentworth—what great rewards both police and criminals would have paid to know that he was the Spider—was working as a common seaman aboard the *Remodo* because he believed he might find on this tramp freighter a clue to the criminal genius whose secret plotting was bringing danger and death to so many citizens of the United States. The destruction of ships at sea was part of the conspiracy and apparently, Wentworth's murder was another!

There had been no difficulty getting a berth aboard the ship. Few seamen cared to sign on a freighter stuffed to the scuppers with explosives as was the *Remodo*. That part had been easy, but

1

for four days while the tramp churned southward, he had studied his companions of the fo'c's'le in vain. Finally he had resorted to an old trick. He had taken the least trustworthy man on board "into his confidence." He had told the sailor that he was a Secret Service man.

Heaven knew the Spider was no agent of the government.

2

The giant new liner *America* had been blown up at sea when the Captain refused to surrender his cargo.

Though many times he had saved the country from havoc and destruction, Washington had posted fabulous rewards for him. But he expected that. He wanted no thanks for his service to humanity, for his crusades of justice, other than the satisfaction of knowing that he had served. The law could not be blamed for its attitude toward him. The Spider did not hesitate to kill a criminal if his death would best serve the ends of justice.

Wentworth smiled grimly. This was one time when the criminal could best serve justice by living. He wanted this creeping killer, drawing steadily closer to his back, to talk not only of the menace to the country but of the danger that he was sure overshadowed this ship. He believed the *Remodo* was doomed to be listed first as overdue and later as missing, as so many ships had been in recent months.

Muscles tensed, Wentworth crouched slightly as the assassin's feet padded closer. Abruptly, the Spider leaped to the left. Just behind the spot he had quitted, the furtive feet landed heavily. A man grunted, slamming against the ship's rail. The point of a knife grated on steel.

With the speed of a tiger's charge, Wentworth whirled and attacked. His pile-driver fist slammed behind the seaman's ear. As the assassin spun beneath the blow, he hammered a left to the jaw.

The man hit the railing, bounced off, went down on his face to the deck. His body jerked convulsively, flopped over on its back. Wentworth dropped to his knees beside him. Now was the time to work on the killer, to force him to talk and reveal the dread plans of which Wentworth had got no more than a hint ashore. He massaged the man's neck, then his hands stiffened and he cursed between his teeth. There was no pulse!

In short seconds Wentworth's groping hands found the reason. The man had fallen on the knife he had intended for the Spider. But Wentworth felt only chagrin at his death. His trick to win a prisoner who could talk had been snatched from him in the moment of victory.

ABRUPTLY, WENTWORTH jerked to his feet, staring narrow-eyed up into the lowering skies. What was that whining note that pierced even the subdued thunder of the waves, through the moan of rusted tackle? His straining gaze could make out nothing in the black smother of the heavens, but louder and louder keened that sound. It was at first thin and distant, but as he listened, it became a shrill whistle, then a shriek! A muffled cry rose to Wentworth's lips. He megaphoned his hands.

"Hard aport!" he shouted toward the bridge. "Douse all lights. A plane! We're being bombed!"

Swift deduction that last. But the Spider knew that danger hovered over the *Remodo* like a black cloud. This plane, far out at sea, was diving upon her without lights, with motors silent as death, no sound warning of its deadly swoop save the wild song of the wind among her wires.

His cry turned the bridge into a madhouse. The bosun shrilled words, piped crazily. Wentworth caught the mate's stentorian bellow faintly against the whip of the wind. He glimpsed the helmsman's face, drawn and startled in the reflected glow of the binnacle, saw the man's sway and shoulder-heave as he spun the wheel.

The Spider's lips were grim. He knew terror gripped those men, as he had intended it should. It would spur them to the swift action which alone could save them. His cry of *bomb* had reminded them that the *Remodo* was crammed with explosives, that the blast of a mere grenade on her decks would rip the steel plates of the hull apart like cardboard.

Tensely Wentworth waited for the ship to answer the helm. Staring upward into the black skies, he slid two automatics from the armpit holsters, crouched ready. Had his warning come in time? Could this ship dodge the death from the heavens? His straining eyes could find no target. All about was utter blackness save where the faint yellow gleam of the ship's lights fell upon the marching seas. Abruptly, they winked into darkness.

Wentworth drew a long shuddering breath, felt with throbbing gladness a continuous beat of spume on his back like hail. He knew what that meant, knew that the ship was keeling over to the bite of her rudder, turning broadside to the seas to dodge the death above. But would it be in time? Or would a single crashing bomb blow the ship to oblivion, wipe out the Spider on the eve of a battle that he was sure held the very destiny of his country in the balance?

The howl of the diving plane mounted until it pierced the eardrums. Suddenly, from the heavens, a white glare of light blazed out, a magnesium flare attached to a small parachute. Wentworth cursed. His guns flamed in his hands. Out of the blackness, into that dazzling light swooped a huge, streamlined shape—the bombing plane!

Then Wentworth's bullets spanged. The magnesium flare blinked out. In its last dying burst of fire, he saw a silvery streak slant downward from the plane. A gasped cry stuck in his throat. That was the bomb! Useless to throw himself to the deck, useless to pour more lead upward into the darkness seeking that plane. If that bomb touched the decks....

The ship staggered and heeled. The muffled thunder of the exploding bomb quivered through the air, beat on Wentworth's skull. Water sloshed across the decks, knocked him prone. He rolled with the wash, strangling with sea water. But inwardly he was cheering. That tower of invisible water that had spewed upon the decks meant only one thing—the bomb had missed! It had exploded harmlessly in the water beside the *Remodo*.

Not until he staggered to his feet again did he realize that in the instant before the bomb let go, he had heard the plane's motors roar into life again. He listened intently, caught the receding buzz. The sound was swallowed instantly in the thunder of the waves, smacking broadside against the ship. She had half completed her turn. A cry jerked Wentworth's eyes aft. It was a thin young voice and it was terrified.

The Spider knew that voice. It was the radio operator with whom he had been in frequent touch during the four days since the *Remodo* had left New York. A shiver of tension rippled through Wentworth's body. Even before he caught the boy's words, the tones told him that here was new horror and peril. He strained his ears.

"Captain Kimmer!" the radio operator was shrieking. *"For God's sake, Captain Kimmer!"*

WENTWORTH RACED toward the bridge, sprang up the steep companionway. At the top he checked abruptly, head just above the deck of the canvas-sheathed walkway. The half-dressed captain, braced in the wheel-house doorway, bent his

7

lantern-jawed face over a sheet of yellow radio message paper. The operator stood white-faced before him. With a convulsive clenching of his fist, Captain Kimmer crumpled the paper. His face worked with anger.

"Put her back on her course, mister," he said to the mate in a thick voice. "Slow speed."

The radio operator spun away. The *Remodo* already was fighting her way head-on into the seas, Wentworth realized, as the logy rolling eased and the old surge and lunge returned. Neither mate nor captain had seen him as he crouched on the companionway. He shrank deep into the shadow of the canvas, his lean face intent.

"What is it, captain?" he heard the mate ask. He could not see him, but Captain Kimmer was in plain sight, standing rigidly. The fist knotted about the radio message was like a mace.

"Pirates!" Kimmer said thickly. "We're ordered to proceed to the lee of Beulah Key, put our cargo overboard in boats and steam away. If we use the radio in the meantime, a bomb will be dropped through our decks. That first bomb was only a warning."

The words beat like pellets of hot lead into Wentworth's brain. Piracy by airplane! That was how all those missing ships—the clue that had put him on this trail—had disappeared. He cursed under his breath, feeling throbbing rage within him. So this was the new menace that threatened his country! There was more to it than piracy, too. His scanty information had indicated that the nation itself was in peril. This was only a single phase of the menace!

A single phase! Good God in Heaven! Then the whole gigantic conspiracy would indeed create a hell upon earth. Careful planning, faultless execution were obvious in this first blow. There was intelligence behind this attack—rare criminal intelligence.

Any captain who plied the seven seas would be forced to obey such an order. The commerce of the world was at the mercy of these men. In a dazzling flash, Wentworth saw the whole fearful possibilities of such a mode of attack. No ship on all the earth would be safe from their depredations! It meant war to the death....

Wentworth slipped back to his post in the bows where the assassin's body rolled laxly to each surge of the ship. With a tight smile on his lips, Wentworth heaved the body overboard, then stood gazing out over the mounting fury of the seas. He was a stalwart, strong-shouldered man just under six feet. His lean face, made leaner and weathered, traced with sun wrinkles by the skilled use of grease paint, was hard set as the steel plates of the ship.

There was anger in the stiff poise of his head, anger at this new menace to long-suffering humanity. A wave slapped the port bow, doused him with flying white water. Another smacked in its wake. The ship was coming about on the course for Beulah Key—and surrender to the pirates.

THE SPIDER frowned as he draped a blue denim sleeve across his sea-wet face. This piracy at sea, menacing as it was, pregnant with great lootings and killings, did not dove-tail with the information that had sent him on this perilous adventure. He thought back swiftly over the events which had sent him voyaging on this death-laden ship in the guise of a common sailor.

When no major outbreaks of crime, no manifestation of some warped master brain plotting against the people came to light for a period, it was Wentworth's practice to seek to anticipate the next attack, to fathom it before most of the world was aware that it impended. Just one week ago tonight, he had gone to the waterfront on such a quest, on the trail of what seemed to him to portend a fearful crime.

A series of steamers had failed to make port, had vanished without even a whisper from their radios. They were, for the most part, small ships without passengers. Newspapers had failed to discover the situation. Wentworth himself had described it only because it was his self-appointed task to ferret out all possible crimes.

Seeking an explanation of these tragedies, Wentworth had assumed a character he had built up carefully, that of Snuffer Dan Tewkes, a Cockney sea-going steward who once every month or so returned to lodgings near the Bowery. Finally in a notorious dive whose back rooms only the ultra-initiate—which included Snuffer Dan Tewkes—could enter, Wentworth had seen a man whose small, smiling face had sent hundreds to their deaths. That man was Remarque D'Enry, promoter of more South and Central American revolutions than could be counted on the fingers of both hands.

What was this man, Wentworth wondered, doing in the underworld haunts of New York?

Unobtrusively, Wentworth maneuvered nearer Remarque

D'Enry, whose delicate hands flew with animated gestures as he talked with two seamen. Only scraps of conversation were audible, but in those had been reiterated time and again the name of the freighter *Remodo*. D'Enry had mentioned also one of the ships that had vanished. In the end Wentworth had gathered that, incredible as it seemed, D'Enry's genius for stirring up insurrections had been called into play against the government of the United States.

An American Revolution was planned! Wentworth stumbled finally from the place in a seemingly drunken wobble, shadowed the revolutionary—and lost him. Nor in the days of feverish search that followed had he been able to locate the man again. Finally, only one course was left open, to ship on the *Remodo* and there trace out the faint trail of revolution, piracy, and death.

He had found it, God knew, and since he had, the *Remodo* could serve him no longer. Somehow he must slip aboard the pirate craft and learn its secrets.

Dully Wentworth heard the bridge bell tinkle, found that he was stiff with cold and the drenching rain of spray. Still pondering his problem, he turned to the big bell behind him, struck out a rhythmic echo. He realized abruptly that he had hit eight bells, that his watch was over. He saw the relief man sway toward him across the pitching deck, and stared a last time out over the sea, graying in the early dawn. Far on the horizon he spotted a dark, low-lying shadow. He cupped his mouth with his hands.

"Land ho!" he sang. "Island three points off port bow!"

THAT WOULD be Beulah Key, he thought swiftly, the pirate rendezvous. He strained his gaze out over the tossing waters, but neither then nor afterward while he and the crew labored to transfer the cargo to the lifeboats did the pirates betray their presence by any sign except the intermittent warning whisper of the radio.

It was broad daylight, a gray, overcast sky, when the *Remodo* steamed finally away from the anchored boats—but Wentworth was not aboard. At the last minute, he had swum to a loaded lifeboat, stowed away beneath the tight tarpaulin that covered it. There he remained while the freighter, riding high for lack of ballast, wallowed off toward the horizon.

Wentworth was in a perilous position, cached in a boat of loot to which pirates would presently come. Yet he intended to remain here, to spy on those pirates, learn their secrets—to destroy ship and men! Only the Spider would have undertaken such a feat, alone and adrift in a boat hundreds of miles from any port. Yet there was a faint smile on his lips as he watched the *Remodo* draw her black plume of smoke toward the horizon. Abruptly, Wentworth stiffened. An oath rose unbidden to his lips. A tight formation of planes was coming out of the south. As he spotted them, one ship whirled from the V, swooped toward the *Remodo*.

The tragedy was over even as Wentworth drew a deep breath. The plane swept high over the ship, then spun off toward its companions. An instant later, the *Remodo* heaved up from the surface of the sea as if an incredible monster had risen beneath her.

Black particles that were parts of the ship—and parts of men—flung skyward amid a sheet of crimson and yellow flame.

A tower of water gushed upward, then there was only a brown cloud of smoke rolling greasily across the surface of the water. The ship had disappeared.

All this happened in dead silence, as if it had been shown in brilliant colors upon a silent motion-picture screen without even the accompaniment of kettle drums, without even the stirring of feet while the audience sat with caught breath.

Nearly two score men had died—lantern-jawed Captain Kimmer with his mighty fists, the white-faced radio operator with his thin eager voice…. Wentworth heard the small patting of waves against the hull of the boat, caught the mewing complaint of a wheeling sea-bird. Finally, awful even in its distance, delayed by space, came the rumbling mutter of the explosion.

Wentworth shuddered and covered his eyes. The Spider had killed many men, had wiped out small armies of criminals, but they had been armed men who could fight, who had earned death a hundred times over. The sailors who had just died were simple brave men of the sea who could not strike back at the beasts that overwhelmed them.

When Wentworth raised his face, his lips were a thin, bitter line like a puckered scar. These men who were coming now in their swift planes to gather their loot, these men who had slaughtered the innocents would find a surprise awaiting them at Beulah Key—a Spider who could sting!

Wentworth laid a hand upon a wooden crate that held nitro-glycerine. His fingers clenched about a corner of it. The knuckles whitened.

13

CHAPTER 2
THE SPIDER'S WEB

FOR SECONDS longer, Wentworth watched the planes, then he went swiftly to work on the box of nitroglycerine, glancing now and again at the ships. They broke formation, slanted one by one to the water.

What manner of men could these be that they killed so ruthlessly? The Spider would find that out, would learn, too, what inspired these fiendish crimes and who were the leaders. But just now, he must prepare his trap. His lips curled back from the gleam of his teeth as he worked with a flashlight battery, a watch, and nitroglycerine. When he finished, it would be a crude, but effective, time bomb! The planes were all on the surface now, taxiing across the calmer waters in the lee of the island, crowding in toward the long line of anchored and loot-laden lifeboats.

Feverishly, Wentworth worked. As his fingers flew, he calculated rapidly to determine how much time he must allow in setting the bomb to explode. It had taken four hours to load the boats; it should take not more than six to load the planes. Six, and a safety margin of an hour and a half. He set the time-bomb to go off in seven and a half hours. Then, just as the planes swung in close, wingtips brushing the tops of the loads, he slipped from under the tarpaulin and slid into the water.

The lifeboats were strung together end to end, and anchored in place. They rose and fell gently on the subdued swells; the planes floated easily with them. Clinging to a rope, peering between two of the boats, Wentworth studied the ships, which were giant Sikorskys. They did not bear the usual numerals on their tails and wings—had no identifying marks. Men climbed out on their wings and the Spider's forehead wrinkled in a perplexed frown. If he had hoped for a clue to the master schemer through the men, he was doomed to disappointment. They were of all races and nationalities.

There was a Chinese among them in a khaki uniform and there was a swarthy Mexican. One had the square head of the Germanic peoples, another the small animated gestures of a Frenchman. Two others just as obviously were Americans.

No, there was nothing here to help him, but—his lips thinned in an ominous smile—when his trap had been sprung, he would find a way to make his prisoners talk. For the time-bomb was not alone intended to punish these men for their ruthless murders. It would also assist the Spider to seize a ship with its entire crew! That done, he would find a way to make them talk!

The Spider nodded once as if in confirmation of the plan, then he drew a deep breath, dived noiselessly beneath the surface of the water. He swam the length of the chain of boats, waited his chance and dived again, coming up this time in the cover of the boat-bottom of one of the Sikorskys. Watching his chance, he scrambled into its cargo compartment, hid among crates of explosives that had already been put aboard. There he lay, through the long hot hours of the day.

It was not until four hours of the seven and a half he had allotted in setting the bomb had elapsed that he began to worry. The men worked with incredible slowness. Wentworth fumed, watched the clock set in the forward wall of the plane, visible to him through a narrow crack in a partition between cabin and cargo compartment. Seven hours had ticked past and Wentworth's weathered face was set in a desperate mold when the motors of the ships finally roared out and one by one the giant Sikorskys left the surface.

Wentworth's ship was the last to rise and when finally it lifted sluggishly into the air, all but fifteen minutes of the seven and a half hours had passed. The stowaway's lips were set, his eyes fixed tensely on the clock as if by his very stare he would detain those flying hands.

In fifteen minutes, the bomb would let go! Tons of explosives would blast the heavens wide open, would hurl five planes to destruction—and with them, the Spider!

HE WAS doomed, and all his hopes of helping his country avoid the fate these men had planned for it were doomed also unless he acted swiftly. Yet he could not act until the Sikorskys gained altitude. The planes were laboring along a scant fifty feet above the seas. Wentworth beat his clenched fist softly on the edge of a munition case.

There were six men in this plane, counting the one at the controls. He would have to overcome them, seize the stick and put hundreds of yards of distance between this plane and those others laden with explosives if his plan was to succeed, if indeed he was to live. Furthermore, he must take at least some of those men alive. It was a stupendous task for a lone man to accomplish at all, but to do it in fifteen minutes....

Yet Wentworth figured there was one chance in a thousand that he might succeed. Feverishly, he ripped open the case nearest him, extracted a lead can of nitroglycerine. The beat of the powerful motors drowned the sound. He tugged an automatic from his sea-soaked clothing, stripped from it the oil-silk covering which had protected it during submersion. Then his disguised face serious, eyes grim, he fingered the narrow door leading through the partition. It was in vain. That door was locked.

Wentworth choked down an oath. His plan for a surprise attack was spoiled; his already meager chances were further reduced. But he must win—he *must!* The door would have to be smashed down. There was no hope that the sound would be drowned by the engine. He would rush in on five armed men who would be forewarned of his coming.

Though it seemed certain suicide, he could not delay. He put the nitro can and gun behind him, slammed his shoulder mightily against the flimsy door. It crashed with a blast like a grenade and Wentworth reeled into the cabin. His eyes were half-dazzled by sunlight streaming through the windows. He made out five men sprawled in seats about the cabin. Before he could speak, one sprang to his feet. His hand streaked toward a holstered gun at his thigh.

Wentworth's automatic spat with instinctive speed, with the accuracy born of years of practice. The lead took the pirate between the eyes, slammed him back across the lap of a companion.

"Freeze!" Wentworth bellowed above the roar of the motors. "Freeze, damn you, or I'll blow us all to hell. This is nitroglycerine in the can!"

He held up the can of nitro and put the muzzle of the automatic against it. Panic stiffened the faces of the four men who twisted in their seats to stare at him. Wentworth gave them only time to see that he actually held a can of explosive, then he barked orders at them. Good Lord, they were slow. The seconds that meant life were zipping past. More than five minutes of his precious fifteen already had sped. In one of those other planes, flying not a hundred feet away, his time-bomb was ticking on toward the ultimate click which would crash them all to death.

"On your feet!" Wentworth snapped. "All of you. On your feet!"

The men reeled up drunkenly, terror-stricken eyes going from the face of this madman with the gun to the can of death in his left hand.

"March toward me," Wentworth ordered next.

At last, after a long moment, they began to move toward him,

Richard Wentworth

their movements a tragic comedy of slow-motion pictures. Each lift of a foot seemed to take hours.

"Hurry, damn you!" he grated.

The first man reeled toward him. Wentworth shrank against the right-hand wall of the plane, watched with glittering eyes.

Would they never pass him? After dragging moments, the last man moved past.

With a gulp of relief, Wentworth reached out and slugged him with his automatic. Before the man had crumpled, the Spider sprang on the next man, struck him down, too, with a swift clip behind the ear. The other two men whirled. Wentworth shook the can of nitro in their faces. With hoarse screams, they fell back.

Once more the gun raked out and now there was only one pirate left on his feet. Desperately, the man's hands darted to the gun that swung against his thigh. Wentworth shot him through the heart, whirled forward even as the man fell. It was ruthless, but these men had slain wantonly—and a horrible death was only seconds away! Ten minutes gone now, and he still had the pilot to account for, still had to send this plane streaking out of formation, to snatch it from the range of the bomb which would rend the sky any moment now.

WENTWORTH RACED toward the bulkhead that shut off the cockpit from the cabin of the plane. Without warning, the door slid aside and the pilot peered back. At sight of Wentworth darting toward him with drawn gun, the pilot's mouth sagged open. He slammed the door. Wentworth ducked aside. A bullet screamed through the thin panel.

Wentworth cursed. The plane was less than a thousand feet above the water. The bomb had less than four minutes to go. He must act at once, yet his only chance of seizing control of the ship was to shoot the pilot. That meant the plane would spin down out of control. There was scarcely space to pull such a huge ship out of its dive. If he succeeded in that, there would be no time left to race to safety before the hell he had planted in its sister plane cut loose.

Yet there could be no hesitation. He must plan and act like greased lightning. Every second he delayed meant a second less in which he could fight off death. Deliberately Wentworth raised his automatic and fired all save his last cartridge through the door at the spot where the pilot sat.

Instantly he plunged toward the door, seized its knob. If he had missed the pilot, if the man had dodged aside, Wentworth was certain to be shot down as he entered. He had saved one shot for that emergency, but even a moment's hesitation now would plunge the plane into the water. The Spider, and his country with him, would be doomed! These thoughts, the swift estimates of danger, flashed through the Spider's brain, but there was no hesitancy in his hand as it yanked the door aside.

As he plunged through the door of the cockpit, diving frantically aside to dodge a possible shot from the pilot, he saw at once that his fusillade had been successful. His bullets had sieved the back of the pilot's head. The last man was out of the way, but even in death, the pilot threatened to destroy him.

The man's dying clutch had yanked back the stick, had thrown the giant ship into a stall! A tail-spin, most perilous of all disasters that threatens ships in the air, would follow. Less than a thousand feet above the sea, Wentworth would have to act with desperate speed, have phenomenal luck, to snatch the plane from that danger. If he succeeded, there would be only seconds left before the blast let go....

21

The wrench as the plane slid off and dived for the ocean threw Wentworth off his feet. Frantically he scrambled up. He seized the dead pilot by the collar; his hands slipped in warm blood. With a cry of despair he could not restrain, the Spider  grasped the dead man by the throat, dragged him from the seat, flung himself at the controls. He glanced at the dials. The Sikorsky had cut its altitude in half. Only five hundred feet from the deadly waters.

Abruptly, the fury of panic left Wentworth. Coolly he kicked the rudder, set about pulling the ship out of its spin. His hands stuck to the wheel. The pilot's life blood had adhered to his palms. He was seconds from disaster—seconds from death—either in the terrific crack up of the plane, or from the explosion that would blast the air for hundreds of yards. But Wentworth's set face was utterly calm.

Gently, he eased the stick backward, gently turned the ailerons against the spin of the Sikorsky. Slowly the ship's nose began to come up. Then with a sick, shuddering violence that seemed to thrust Wentworth's stomach down into his legs, the ship zipped out of the spin so close to the wave tops that its hull slapped up spray. It smeared the window before Wentworth's eyes.

How many seconds now before that time bomb ripped the heavens apart? Wentworth darted a glance at the instrument panel-clock. Thirty seconds! He stared upward. The other planes were almost directly above him, swinging in a wide circle, watching his staggering dive to the sea. One of those ships held death for all of them. Thirty seconds—less than that now! He could not put enough distance between himself and that death-bearer for safety. The blast would drive his ship into the waves....

THERE WAS only one thing to do. Despite those mountainous seas, those sliding dark hills of water, he must set his plane down. If he were resting on the surface at the time of the explosion, at least the fall would not wreck him. He would have a chance.

Wentworth cut the powerful engines, began skimming the wave tops with consummate skill, touching one, lifting a few inches, touching the top of another.

His speed lessened quickly. Abruptly Wentworth pulled up the nose of the giant ship and stalling, pancaked it on the down-slant of a wave. It lifted as the next huge roller swept under it, started to twist broadside. Wentworth gunned the motors, fought with the rudder. The ship straightened nose-on into the seas. Barely had he achieved that maneuver when the skies split above his head—the time bomb and nitroglycerine had let go.

Wentworth was gazing straight ahead when the blast struck. It seemed to him that the waters were flattened out by the concussion. The tops of the waves broadened, spread out into the valleys; white caps vanished. It was the impression of an instant, then his skull was thunder-beaten. Crushing weights slammed against his ears. He gasped, laboring for breath, and the giant Sikorsky seemed to squat down on the water. A green wall rose before him, and fighting a feeling of helpless inertia in his arms, Wentworth gunned the motors and ruddered the ship nose-on.

The wave broke over the ship with the thunder of a second blast. The motors coughed, spluttered. They groaned with the weight on the propellers, labored as if bursting. Then the wave had passed. The ship rode lightly on the crests of the rollers and the motors spluttered an instant longer, then burst into a steady, deep-throated hum.

Wentworth tilted back his head and stared up through the yellowed glass overhead into the sky. He was instantly aware that only fractions of a second had elapsed since the blast. Three of the planes were still in the air, plunging toward the seas. The fourth had simply vanished, disintegrated by the explosion. That one had carried the time-bomb.

The other three black blobs against the sky were identifiable as planes only because Wentworth knew there had been three more ships in the air. They were crumpled, twisted pieces of metal. In them, the explosives miraculously had not let go, but the force of the mighty blast from their sister ship had smashed them out of all recognition. Wings had been ripped off, tail-groups destroyed, cabins caved in upon themselves. As Wentworth watched, his Sikorsky heaved to the crest of a mountainous wave and he saw the shattered ships smack into the water. Towers of spray rose, then sprinkled down lazily, brushed by the wind. The sun broke through the clouds and made a rainbow dance for a moment on the crests. Then that too, was gone. The *Remodo* was avenged.

CHAPTER 3
THE SPIDER IS CAPTURED

BUT WENTWORTH was under no illusion that he had defeated the pirates by this initial skirmish. He had blocked their access to supplies, destroyed planes, but somewhere the leaders still existed. And the Spider was in perilous straits. Men behind him had been only knocked out, ruthless men who did not hesitate to wipe out an entire ship with its crew. Furthermore Wentworth dared not for an instant desert his post at the controls, lest the thundering waves destroy this frail craft. The Sikorsky was never built for stormy seas. It shuddered at each slap of flying spray.

It would be impossible to rise again from these waters. His only hope was to taxi back to the lee of Beulah Key where smoother seas would permit a take-off. That would take at least an hour of careful maneuvering. Meantime, those men behind him would regain consciousness. It would take them seconds only to overpower him, handicapped as he was by the necessity of keeping hands and brain on the task of combatting the seas. Only by keeping precisely nose-on to the charge of waves could they survive.

The plane pitched sickeningly on the rollers, climbed gray mountains of water, slid down their sides as if she would plunge straight to the bottom. Each descent into the valley was a battle with death—a battle that would be lost if for a second Wentworth ceased to hold the prow straight into the coming waves. As it was, her nose ploughed into the angry waters, lifted reluc-

25

tantly. Only the steady slow drumming of the propellers kept life in the Sikorsky.

Wentworth glanced anxiously behind him. The pilot lay where he had been tossed, crumpled against the thin partition that separated cockpit from cabin. Four bullets had smashed through the back of his head. His face... Wentworth grimaced. Soft-nosed bullets at close range.

He peered back through the doorway. Only one of the three men he had left alive in the back compartment was visible. He rolled as limply as a newly-made corpse to the toss and pitch of the plane. A gleam came to Wentworth's eyes. He had caught the glint of a metallic symbol on the collar of the man's khaki tunic. It indicated the man was a pilot. If he could revive him ahead of the others, keep him under control—but Wentworth shrugged, realizing that he could not leave the cockpit.

His lips lifted in a brief smile, wrinkling the leathery face that he had manufactured upon his own. He made a queer figure in his soggy seaman's clothes, steadily maneuvering the plane. The intelligence of his blue-gray eyes made a startling contrast. The gleam in them grew. He had hit upon a plan!

Holding the plane to her course with his feet upon the rudder, Wentworth took from the toolkit he always carried strapped under his left arm a length of silken cord. It was made of the finest quality material and though not so large in diameter as a lead pencil, it tested at 700 pounds. He made a loop of this, working with practiced hands while his eyes watched the tremendous marching waves.

Once more he snatched a glance back through the narrow

door. The man had tossed against a chair, and a limp-wristed hand was thrust upward. Wentworth weighted his looped silken cord swiftly with a ring of keys twisted about and lassoed that upthrust hand.

A glance ahead showed the next wave was a cross-sea, running at a slight angle. Wentworth spun the plane to meet this new peril, then once more he had a space of seconds to work. He twisted the silk about his fists, drew the line over his shoulders, and heaved forward from the waist. Minutes of back-breaking toil and his prisoner lay beside him.

WENTWORTH LIFTED the plane over the next wave, looked down upon his catch. The man's face was dour and dark. Even in unconsciousness, it seemed malevolent. The open mouth had tight, secretive lines about its corners; the nose was sharp and long.

As Wentworth watched him, guiding the plane with his feet from the feel of the seas that slid under her, the man breathed a half groan, moved his head jerkily. The lips closed drily, opened again. The eyelids fluttered, flew wide—and the man looked into the muzzle of Wentworth's gun.

"Just lie there," the Spider ordered shortly. He told the man briefly that the plane was doomed unless her nose was kept into the seas and ordered him to take charge. A small, sneering smile twisted the man's impressed lips.

"Like hell I will," he rasped. "We'll just wait until my friends come to and take you—Or the other planes…" He stared up suddenly through the overhead glass, saw only empty sky. "In God's name!" he cried hoarsely. "Where are the other ships?"

"I blew them up," said Wentworth. The smile that brushed his lips was cold. Without a word, he leveled the automatic at the man's head. Panicked eyes widened as the Spider's trigger-finger whitened.

"For God's sake!" the man gasped. "You wouldn't shoot me in cold blood?"

Wentworth's smile did not alter. "It isn't cold blood," he drawled softly. "This is self-defense. If I don't kill you now, you will presently help your friends kill me. If you think I won't shoot, just turn your head to the left a bit."

The man stared up into the coldly calm eyes of the Spider; his tongue-tip slid out to lick dry lips. He turned his head slowly to the left. His eyes held to Wentworth's even as his head moved. Then he perked their gaze briefly to what once had been his fellow-pilot's face. A choked cry rose to his lips. His look flew back to Wentworth and there was horror in it.

"Will you take over the controls?" the Spider asked again.

The man's head jerked in a fearful affirmative. He eased to a sitting position, eyes sliding fearfully toward his dead friend.

"Stand up," Wentworth ordered tensely and the man obeyed. "Now then, come here beside me, but remember, if you so much as touch my arm, I'll shoot. And while we struggle, the ship will go down."

He waited until the plane was climbing sluggishly up a wall of gray water, ducked from the seat, thrust the other man violently into place, saw him grip the controls competently. He found the man's gun, took another from the dead pilot.

"Just keep her nose into the seas," he said, "and you'll be all right."

He left the cockpit. That dour-faced man at the controls was chained to his seat as securely as if fetters of steel restrained him. Swiftly Wentworth disarmed the men who remained alive, bound them to chairs. He dragged the corpses aft, seated them so they faced the two he had bound. Then upon the forehead of each corpse, he pressed the base of a small cigarette-lighter he slipped from his pocket.

When he removed the lighter, there gleamed on the forehead of the three who were dead a small vermillion spot, a symbol of sprawling hairy legs and vicious fangs, *the seal of the Spider!*

Then he returned to the cockpit. Following Wentworth's instructions, the impressed pilot turned the Sikorsky's tail to the seas and with wind and motors pushing, made a slow and cautious retreat to the lee of Beulah Key. An hour and a half after Wentworth had blasted the pirates from the skies, the Sikorsky was in the air again, winging westward toward the distant mainland of the United States.

During the long flight back, Wentworth ceaselessly questioned the prisoners, but even face-to-face with the vengeance of the Spider, as printed upon the foreheads of dead friends, they would not talk.

Wentworth became convinced finally that they knew nothing. He returned to the cockpit and far ahead spotted a low-lying dark cloud that was land.

"The gasoline's about out," the pilot told him shortly.

Wentworth glanced at the gauge, peered ahead at the tracery

29

of land lifting from the sea. "Put her down as close to that beach as possible," he ordered and stood ready with his gun. The dark cloud divided itself into the glossy green of foliage and the white gleam of sandy beach. The Sikorsky kissed the cobalt waters that here gave only a hint of the turmoil of Beulah Key.

As the nose of the plane settled, Wentworth dropped a loop of rope over the pilot's shoulders and arms, jerked it tight and bound him to the seat.

THE MAN made no resistance, but there a gleam in his eyes that the Spider, busy with the ropes, missed—a mocking hard gleam of raw hatred and triumph! He wiped it off his face as Wentworth straightened from his task, and leaning across him worked rudder and throttle until the plane beached, with a heeling jerk.

"You won't have to stay this way very long," Wentworth assured him. "This is the mainland of Florida and before many hours have passed, the police will take you."

The man looked at him without words and this time Wentworth caught the mocking glitter of his eyes. He only smiled at its hatred, waved a sardonic farewell and waded ashore. There was a break in the moss-draped palms. Wentworth ploughed heavily through the deep white sand. The sun was low in the west. Within short minutes the sudden tropic night would drop its black curtain. Before then, Wentworth must have summoned the police or the coast guard to the plane. The stolen explosives she carried would convict the pirates. He himself must race back to New York, to pick up the trail of Remarque D'Enry again. He had struck a blow at the pirates but their leaders still eluded him. Without some clue to their identity, he could not hope to check their plans. Authorities would be helpless....

Wentworth crossed the white beach, plunged into the half-shade of the palms. His eyes were dazzled with brilliance, his ears deadened by hours of drumming motors. Yet some sixth sense seemed to spot danger. He sprang backward, hand snaking to his gun. A blow smashed down on his shoulder!

The Spider whirled, firing. A man screamed with his death wound. More blows rained upon Wentworth's head and shoulders. A club caught his wrist, knocked the pistol from his numbed hand. Another bludgeon hammered him to his knees.

"Don't kill him," a voice rasped. "I think the *señor* has things to tell us."

Wentworth fought to his feet. Men were all about him. Good Lord, had he walked into a nest of pirates? He must escape and—

A blast of white pain spurted through his brain. He felt himself falling, felt the hot bite of sun-warmed sand grinding into his face, then all sensation vanished in a flood of hot, light-shot darkness. His final thought was of the gleam in the captive pilot's eyes. He knew, in that last moment, that somehow the man had tricked him. He was in the hands of the Pirates!

CHAPTER 4
PIRATE MERCY

A S WENTWORTH fell to the white sand in the gloom of the palm grove, a short man with a villainous

A fist like iron raked under the leader's chin, caught him on the larynx. His words were choked off in his throat.

face sprang toward his prostrate body. He carried a heavy club and standing astride the helpless Spider, he raised that club high above his head with both hands. His teeth showed in an evil grin. His purpose was clear. When he smashed down with that club, he would cave in Wentworth's head like a melon.

The club started downward, then checked in mid-stroke. The man screamed. His arms stiffened, seemed stricken with a strange and instantaneous paralysis. Something sinuous had licked out of the gloom.

It had slapped softly upon the man's wrists and coiled about them like a snake.

Now, as the man stood screaming and helpless, as the club fell impotently from his hands and struck the sand with a soft thud, a wide-shouldered giant of a man sprang from the gloom. He held a short handled whip in his hands. It was the lash of this whip that had twined about the vicious killer's wrists. The handle flicked backward and the whip's prisoner pitched to the earth.

"I said, 'Let him live,'" the big man admonished.

Three other men shrank back from around Wentworth. Upon the ground lay the man the Spider had slain and the one who writhed with his hands in the vise of the whip. The big man twitched the handle and the whip came free. He coiled it slowly about his forearm; it was fully fifteen feet long. He finished with that before he spoke again.

"Miguel! Juan!" he said in Spanish, "Carry this prisoner to the house. Jesus! José! Go to the plane and see why our men did not also disembark. Take this carrion with you."

With his toe, he touched the man Wentworth had slain, then paused. The man who had fallen prisoner to the whip felt his eyes upon him, got to his knees, held up his arms in silent petition—"José *mío*," said the leader, "see that thou obeyest orders next time or thou wilt taste of the whip—*in another way!*"

The man José bowed shuddering to the ground and the big man turned, strode back along the trail. Despite his broad height, he moved with a certain alien grace. Stepping from the shade of the palms into the red last rays of the sun, he revealed himself in long loose-legged white ducks, a shirt open at the throat. The whip dangled from his wrist by a thong, a coil of flat plaited leather. His head was bare and the reddish hair upon it bristled straight upward in a ruff.

Behind him, two Mexicans toiled with Wentworth, swinging him between them limply. They stumbled into the cabin and at the orders of their leader bound the Spider with coils of rope. The tropic night fell while they labored; a candle thrust into the neck of an empty rum bottle was lighted on the table. Behind this sat the leader, elbows heavily on it, brawny forearms clasped loosely together, the whip sprawled out beside them.

The leader's face was craggy and thickly scarred by smallpox. He had a square heavy jaw and Irish blue eyes—arrogance in that thin, high-bridged nose, cruelty in the lean, firm-pressed lips. This was Miguel Oriano whose father had been a swash-buckling soldier of fortune by the name of Mike O'Ryan who had carved a minor kingdom among the peons of Mexico.

Oriano looked up sharply at a rapid thudding of feet in the darkness. Three men stormed into the cabin door. The first was the dour-faced pilot.

"Where is he?" he demanded with a searing oath. "Where is that son of unspeakable parents?"

He spotted Wentworth, strode on long, loose-kneed legs toward him, drew back a heavy boot in front of his face.

"Stop!" spoke Miguel Oriano. He said it quietly enough, hand carelessly on the coils of his whip. The foot checked-in mid-blow; the gaunt pilot spun about.

"You don't know what this man did," he said violently. "Hell, Oriano! He's the Spider!"

ORLANO CHUCKLED. The sound was deep but not in the least humorous. "Well, the Spider is well trussed," he said, in the same soft, slightly accented tones. "Presently we will dispose of him. But first there are certain questions to be asked. Tell me, what did he do?"

"What did he do?" the pilot almost screamed.

He strode to the table, put both hands on its edge and leaned forward. When he spoke, his lanky body bobbed from the waist, "He blew up four of our planes, destroyed the loot of the *Remodo,* and killed twenty-seven of our men!"

Oriano ripped to his feet. The crude chair on which he sat thunder-bolted back against the wall and splintered. The leader stood staring fixedly at the pilot, his great craggy face thrust forward, chest heaving with ragged breath, hand knotted about his whip. The candle flame leaped high with the violence of his movements, then quivered on its wick.

"He shall die," Oriano rasped, *"by the whip!"*

He gusted breath from his pumping lungs, sent it whistling through his nostrils. When he spoke again, his voice was once more calm and liquid. "But first there must be questions," he said. "Tell your story, Norska."

He turned slowly to the broken chair, shrugged at the fragments and draped a thigh across a corner of the table. It creaked with his weight.

The pilot, Norska, told of Wentworth's attack. "After he put me in charge of the plane," he concluded, "I faked the dial to look like the gasoline supply was giving out, then when we slanted down toward the cabin—toward which I had been heading all the time—I flashed our riding lights on and off in Morse code. Luckily one of you caught that and the rest you know."

Oriano got slowly from the table and with his boot-toe rolled Wentworth over on his back. The disguised sailor face that the Spider has assumed stared up at him with closed eyes. The leader shook his head.

"I still don't see," Oriano said slowly, "how this animal found out about the *Remodo*. We will question him a bit before I begin the real work with the whip."

He drew back his foot, smashed it against Wentworth's side. As he struck his lips snarled back from whitely perfect teeth. He laughed then, a softly liquid, even beautiful sound.

"Come, *señor,* " he said, "open your eyes. An unconscious man does not wince from a blow."

Wentworth opened his eyes, staring upward into the craggy, pock-marked face of Miguel Oriano. Even if he had not, under the cover of assumed unconsciousness, heard most of the pilot's story, he would have known that death awaited him here.

Already the Spider had tested his ropes, discovered that unless someone other than himself loosened them, he was hopelessly a prisoner. He was wrapped in manila line like a cocoon. It bit painfully into his wounds of battle, but he smiled debonairly at Miguel Oriano, whose gaze was no longer puzzled. He had looked in Wentworth's eyes.

"That is better," Oriano mused quietly.

Wentworth glanced about the room. The flickering candle threw weird shadows over the walls of palmetto logs beneath a thatched roof. Besides the leader, there were seven men in the

37

room, the four Mexicans and the three from the plane. Wentworth's eyes sought out Pilot Norska.

"You were clever," be said conversationally. "It is not given to many to outwit the Spider."

No smile touched the in-pressed lips of Norska; his black gaze glowered at the bound man. "You're not so tough," he rasped.

"Not tough, no," Oriano agreed softly, "but clever. *Por Dios,* yes. How, *Señor* Spider, did you ever discover our plans against the *Remodo?*"

A FLEETING smile brushed Wentworth's lips.

While he played at words with these men, he was thinking desperately. Death already was reaching out its bony arms to embrace him—death by the fiendish torture of the whip. But that was not what Wentworth thought. He wasted not a moment of worry for himself; he had only a passing second of regret that, dying here, he would never again behold the sweet smile of Nita van Sloan, who alone among women knew his secret and had fought with him through months and years of death-defying peril. His thoughts as always were of humanity and what horrors it must suffer as he perished miserably here.

For no one, save the Spider, knew of this new grave peril that lifted its vile head to menace the world, to strike at the country he loved. If he died these demon killers undoubtedly would strike again and again, stealing millions in loot, sending thousands to unmarked watery graves from which their accusing eyes and lips would never rise to name their murderers.

Well, he had a system for getting out of even such fearful traps as this, a system that depended on his incredibly keen brain, on his super-trained body and mental reflexes. The system was simple. First, he never despaired—second, "one thing at a time."

The first barrier to escape was the rope that bound him. He already knew that it would be impossible for him to remove it. Therefore he must force his enemy to free him. When that had been accomplished, he would see what next was to be done....

"Come," said Miguel Oriano, impatience creeping into his voice. "How did you discover our plans against the *Remodo?*"

"Mil perdones, señor," Wentworth said, in a voice made cheerful with effort, "A thousand pardons, but I'm afraid you'll have to guess at the answer."

Oriano stared down at him, his lips lifted slightly from his teeth.

"I have ways, *Señor* Spider," he said softly, "of making men talk."

Wentworth rolled his head from side to side. "They will be useless upon me," he said negligently. "Other men—more skillful—have tried to make me talk and failed."

Deliberately he was goading this man to torture him, goading a man upon whose face cruelty and ruthlessness were written large.

"Are you familiar, *señor,* with the bullwhip?" Oriano asked gently.

Wentworth smiled contemptuously. "A crude device."

"Crude?" Oriano, too, was smiling now—smiling with anticipation. He opened his mouth and boomed out sudden deep laughter. "Crude? Perhaps, *Señor*, but I have found it very effective."

He continued to look down at Wentworth with something very like affection in his hard blue eyes. A man after Oriano's own heart, this Spider. It was to be hoped he would not wilt too soon beneath the lash.

"Juan! Miguel!" he snapped out in Spanish. "To the whipping post!"

TWO PEONS seized Wentworth, one grasping his feet, the other seizing his hands with difficulty beneath the prisoner's bound-down arms. They carried him toward the door.

"I'll be seeing you," Wentworth called back, almost gaily.

"You will," Miguel Oriano answered grimly, *"pronto,* right away."

He strode after the two who carried Wentworth. Another Mexican snatched up a lantern, lighted it, walked beside the two who half-dragged the Spider toward the palms. Weird shadows danced. The drapings of Spanish moss on the trees were like funeral palls.

Beside a palm to which a cross-piece had been lashed they halted Wentworth stared up the slanting trunk. They would tie his wrists to that cross-piece, one hand on each end. His body would be strained up on his toe-tips, dragged forward so that he nearly straddled that slanting trunk. Then the lash would whistle through the night air and bite cruelly into his naked flesh.

A slight smile that was far from mirroring his true feeling crossed Wentworth's lips. Oriano laughed aloud at the prospect of prey for his whip. Wentworth had seen men who had felt that agony. If they survived, they were broken trembling wrecks. That snaky lash would strip the flesh from a man's back, dig into the writhing muscles. A cunning man handling it could crack vertebrae.

"Unroll our butterfly from his cocoon," Oriano said softly. "I do not believe he could enjoy himself while those coils interpose between his flesh and my—*caress!*"

Wentworth had to mask his eyes to hide his exultation. He had calculated that to torture him with the whip, it would be necessary to unwrap the ropes. For a fraction of a second, his hands might be free. He rolled his head toward Oriano, grinned up at the cruelty-warped face. Since first he had laid eyes on the man, had heard the queer contradiction of his soft voice, seen that whip coiled on his arm, a memory had been pecking at his brain. Somewhere he had heard of a hell-driver such as this, and now he had placed him.

Wentworth knew the man's attention must be distracted from the work of the peons. It was a slim chance the Spider had at best.

He turned his head toward Oriano. "I know you," he said steadily, "you are Miguel Oriano."

Oriano's face lighted up at his words.

"So you have heard of me?" His pride was inflated.

Wentworth's voice was dry. "Yes, I have heard of you, Miguel Oriano," he drawled. "You would have been Mike O'Ryan back in the old country if your father hadn't decided a half-breed son would do well enough."

The smile froze on Oriano's face. That term *half-breed* stung him to black fury. He cursed and the whip slashed through the air, cut across Wentworth's chest. Even through the blanket of imprisoning ropes, the lash hurt cruelly, but it won Oriano only a gay laugh from his prisoner.

"Hurts, eh, Miguel *mío*," Wentworth gibed, addressing him familiarly as if he were a peon. "But you see, if thy blood were pure instead of mixed, thou wouldst not have this streak of insanity in thy veins, this desire to torture men."

"Hurry!" Oriano snapped at the Mexicans, "Have you sticks for fingers?" He whirled the whip until it whistled through the air. He rolled the long lash off into the darkness and it cracked like a gun shot.

"Hurry, my children, I grow impatient," chanted Oriano. "My whip grows thirsty."

THE PEONS hurried, fumbling knots loose, jerking at the ropes. They freed first Wentworth's feet, then worked up past his hips, began to uncoil the fibers about his body.

The ropes were off his arms now. Wentworth's blood sang and throbbed with hope. The odds were eight-to-one—eight armed men against one without a weapon—but at least he could fight! He stirred woodenly as if the pressure of his bonds had paralyzed his muscles.

"Hurry," snapped Oriano, "Up with him! To the cross!"

The Mexicans snatched Wentworth's wrists, heaved him from the ground. It was the Spider's chance, the moment for which he had been playing. He came to his feet with a rush, yanking so the two who held him prisoner were wrenched toward the ground. Before they had fallen, Wentworth was in action.

Oriano had time to bellow only the first words of a startled order when the whirlwind of the Spider's attack struck him. A fist like iron raked under the leader's chin, caught him on the larynx. His words were choked off in his throat. His hands flew high and he went reeling backward. His mouth was wide, gasping for breath that would not flow through his paralyzed throat. As he staggered, Wentworth caught the whip and broke the thong that held it with a fierce yank. He sprang sideways toward the peon who held the lantern.

The man dropped the light, hand snatching for the heavy-bladed *machete* at his belt. By the last glimmer of illumination before the lantern crashed, Wentworth flung a swift glance around. The two peons were struggling to their feet, murderous *machetes* bared. The three men he had captured in the plane were grabbing for their guns. Oriano, gripping his throat, was feeble on his feet, but recovering swiftly.

The light went out. Wentworth whirled the long whip in a slow circle above his head and swished its fifteen-foot lash straight at the faces of the men with the guns. In the darkness they could not see it coming, but they heard its hissing song. A frightened cry burst from one, then a scream of anguish.

Wentworth leaped ten feet to his left, swung the lash again, this time toward the two peons who had snatched out *machetes*. Pistol flame spurted from two guns to his right, but they were firing toward the spot where he had stood. By the light of the powder flame Wentworth made out the two Mexicans rushing in with hungry knives. Then the whip streaked forward, hit.

Wentworth threw his shoulders into a backward heave and a man's startled scream of pain choked off.

Oriano bellowed hoarsely for lights. Like an echo, the beam of a flashlight streaked out from the gunman. It spotted a peon, writhing on the ground with the whip's lash twined tight about his throat. It traced the course of the whip, found the handle lying on the ground where the Spider had dropped it. Then, with a smack of metal meeting metal, the light went out.

"Jesus!" a man shrieked. "The Spider's got a *machete!*"

Wentworth whirled the heavy knife he had snatched from the peon felled with the whip. The same stroke which had smacked the flashlight to the earth slashed at the man who held it. The Spider felt the blade gash flesh, heard it grate on bone. The man he had struck groaned hoarsely; his weight sagged on the *machete.* Wentworth could not jerk the weapon clear. He swore softly, wrenched at the handle.

Brilliant blue-white light blazed forth, illuminating the strip of woods like day. A magnesium flare had been lighted. Wentworth leaped to the cover of a palm tree and saw Oriano rush from the flare which he had set, snatch up his whip. With a quick flip of the lash, he freed the end from about the peon's neck. That man did not move; he had been strangled to death.

Wentworth glanced fleetingly about the clearing. Norska was on his knees, hands pressed to the left side of his face. Blood seeped out between his fingers. At Oriano's shout, Norska lifted his head. He dropped his hands, and Wentworth saw, with a quivering of nausea in his stomach, the horror that the whip had wrought in the dark. The man's left eye had been cut from its socket, the whole side of his face was laid open to the bone. A second man from the plane was doubled up on his knees, his head on the earth. The handle of Wentworth's *machete* protruded from his left side. The blade had sliced through his belly and wedged tight in his backbone.

THESE THINGS Wentworth saw in a lightning quick glance, saw also that there was no weapon within reach and that the remaining five men were rallying about Oriano. The leader's hoarse shouts directed the search. Two peons darted through the woods to guard the plane. The other men, guns in hand, walked slowly and cautiously toward the trees that concealed Wentworth.

Wentworth faded away from behind the palm, loped a dozen soft strides into the woods and shinnied up the slanting trunk of another tree. When the hunting party passed beneath him, he was completely hidden in the basket top of a coconut palm. A grim smile twitched across his lips. A single swift throw with a coconut would fell Oriano, But the moment afterward, Wentworth knew, his perch would be riddled with lead. That was a pleasure he would have to forego—for the present.

He waited until the men had crept past toward the sea. Then he slid swiftly down the trunk, hastened back toward the cabin. From the plane, he had spotted a road that wound toward a distant village. If he could reach that place and sound the alarm, not even the Sikorsky, supposing it had fuel enough to fly far, could escape. He could speed army planes upon their trail, hasten police to the scene.

At the clearing, he stopped a moment beside the bodies of

the two men he had slain. His cigarette lighter rested briefly on the forehead of each. If Oriano's men returned here, they would have something to worry about in the brief while before police swept down upon them. They would find upon the foreheads of their dead companions *the seal of the Spider!*

The seals affixed, Wentworth tightened his belt, swung off at a dog-trot through the thick growth of palms toward the road he had spotted and the village beyond. As he jogged along, head thrown back, deep chest pumping rhythmically, his mind flashed on ahead to the tasks that confronted him.

Miguel Oriano was a leader of the pirates, but Wentworth did not believe he was the chief. Oriano was a good man for his task—a merciless driving villain who had scourged half the countries of the world—a trained revolutionist with a past including many more heinous vices and crimes, but he lacked the vision to plot this wholesale piracy, Wentworth was convinced. If the Spider had believed this man alone headed the gang, he would have remained in the wood, unarmed though he was, until he had wiped out this threat to humanity.

But such a course might well have proved the death of the Spider and reckoning that there were other greater hands to fall before this conspiracy would be smashed, he deemed it best to escape, to let police finish off this branch of the gang and return himself to the scene of battle in New York. It was there he had got the first vague clue to this infamous plot. It was there too, that he had heard hints of brewing insurgency within the United States. The threat to the shipping of the world was grave, but this menace to the country of his nativity, the country which above all things he loved, was greater. That was the foe the Spider must battle.

He phoned an alarm to Miami from a village, but when police sought the man who had told of piracy on the high seas—told where to trap the pirates—they could not find the informer anywhere. Wentworth had abandoned his sailor's garb, even then was on his way to Miami in the guise of a traveling salesman.

CHAPTER 5
THE TRAIL OF DOOM

T HIRTEEN HOURS later, when Wentworth alighted at Newark Airport from the plane which sped him from Miami to the New Jersey field which serves New York City, the horror of the piracy at sea was no longer a hearsay matter, revealed only by an anonymous telephone call. It was a fact which the newspapers blazoned with eight-column scareheads across their front pages.

The giant new liner, *America*, largest ever to fly the United States flag, had been blown up at sea when the captain refused to obey a radio command from an airplane that he surrender all his cargo. The bomb had ploughed through the decks, wrecked the engine room. A hundred had been killed by its blast. Within four minutes after that time, the *America* had sunk, carrying down her captain and all except fourteen women and three sailors who had managed to lower a lifeboat in four slim minutes of grace.

The *America* had had time to flash a single SOS, then the bomb that smashed her engines crippled her radio also and the world had not learned the fearful details of the tragedy until this day when The *H.M.S. Olympia,* rushing to the rescue, had picked up the women and sailors.

The toll of dead was over two thousand. The loss in cargo was millions; the civilized world rocked with the horror of this deliberate murder by aerial pirates. Wentworth stared at the headlines, skimmed through the tale of horror with fury seething in his veins. He sat with clenched fists then, gazing with unseeing eyes straight ahead of him. He had struck a blow at these monsters, but it had been feeble, it appeared. They still had strength enough to murder two thousand humans for loot.

Wentworth knew that this act of horror had been committed as a warning to other captains to surrender without quibble. He knew that the warning would be heeded, that hereafter loot would be surrendered without hesitancy by masters who held the human cargo of their vessels dearer than the merchandise which filled their hulls.

He saw before him an unending vista of death and destruction. And this—the piracy at sea—was a minor issue. There was the attack on the government of the United States that pended. In heaven's name, what master mind, what inscrutable genius of horror and crime could be behind this hell?

Wentworth swore grimly, as his cab sped from the Holland Tunnel into the crowded streets of New York, that he would track down and slay this murderer of thousands. But even the Spider could not imagine the full horror, the incredible ingenuity of the killer!

Through a city stunned by the awful calamity that had

befallen the *America*, Wentworth sped directly to Riverside Tower, high above the Hudson River, where Nita van Sloan had her apartment. He strove to put aside thoughts of peril as he rose in the elevator without being announced. A little smile came and went upon his lips, as he sounded their private signal upon the bell—twice short, a third time long. Scarcely had the third peal sounded than a furious barking broke out within and he heard Nita's feet flying to the door.

She flung it wide, held out her two white hands to him, a gay smile on her lips. Wentworth gathered her into his arms. A Harlequin Great Dane wriggled his huge body past them and pawed at Wentworth's leg. He was prancing like a puppy, a whine of eagerness in his throat. Wentworth dropped a hand to his head.

"Howdy, Apollo," he said and the dog writhed and pranced anew. Wentworth laughed at the puppy antics of the 170-pound Great Dane whose shoulders reached almost to his master's waist, then, an arm still about Nita, he walked on into the apartment.

This was the Spider's homecoming. It was always thus, as if he had come back from the dead, that Nita greeted him. For Wentworth's every venture into the streets was a defiance of death itself, so many were his enemies among the underworld, so fierce and strong were the men he battled.

Wentworth made his face calm as he strolled about Nita's apartment idly, coaxed a few chords from the concert grand-piano that filled one corner of the large duplex studio-living room, rested a hand upon his beloved violin. Deliberately fighting

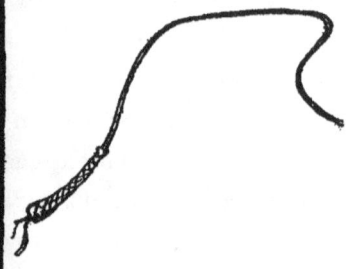

off the thoughts of death and disaster, of the criminals who might be at this instant closing in upon him, he was stealing a few moments of happiness from his life of daily peril.

Nita and he could never marry, not while crime remained to be suppressed, while police had a price upon his head. Wentworth would not involve Nita, would not bring children in the world to suffer the onus that would descend upon them if ever, as was hourly possible, the police should finally learn his identity and hail him before the courts as a criminal for

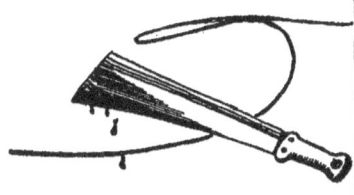

any one of his hundred kills. So he must forego his happiness that he might shield others, might give them the happiness he was denied.

ABRUPTLY, WITH a sharp gesture of his hand, Wentworth ended their brief moment. Stern-faced, jaw firmly set, he crossed to the woman he loved, looked deeply into her blue eyes. He touched the chestnut and gold of her curling hair, smiled briefly.

"You know from the newspapers, of course, what developed on the *Remodo,*" he said. "What's been done here?"

Nita told him swiftly her activities and those of his faithful Hindu servant,

Ram Singh. The Hindu had finally picked up the trail of the revolutionist, Remarque d'Enry, whose saloon talk had sent Wentworth aboard the *Remodo*. The revolutionist had left his water-front haunts for the grandeur of the *Hotel St. Delroy*. The two seamen with whom he had talked had vanished.

"We will call on D'Enry tonight, you and I," Wentworth told Nita. "Meantime, I'll drop in to see the police, and to tell Washington what I have learned...."

He waved a hand. There were a thousand inquiries to make today. Miguel Oriano's description must be broadcast.

When evening fell, Wentworth and Nita went to dine and dance at the *St. Delroy*. It was late when they strolled into the wide-flung roof-garden with its walls and ceiling of plate glass through which drifted the glimmer of the stars. All about them small tables bore subdued roseate lights. An orchestra strummed; softly couples revolved on a dance floor that was the reverse of the old night-club era. It afforded ample room for all.

The headwaiter bowed low before them, recognized Wentworth by name, and led them deftly to a small table upon the edge of the dance floor. Wentworth and Nita exchanged smiles as if they had not a care in the world. Her hands were clasped beneath her chin, with her bare, shapely arms poignant against the deep wine-red of her dress. But these two were deadly serious under the surface. The Spider was on the trail.

"Just across the floor, Dick," said Nita.

Wentworth presently looked where her deep blue eyes had indicated, saw a party of five, three men and two women, at dinner. He recognized at once the small smiling face, the quick gestures of D'Enry, seated between the two women. D'Enry leaned toward a girl gowned entirely in white and Wentworth saw the quick gleam of the man's teeth as he smiled, saw the girl tilt back her head in laughter.

Wentworth was studying the others at the table when another quick-moving figure, stalking across the dance floor, caught his eye. A man was striding directly toward the table. There was something familiar about the abrupt roll of the man's shoulders, that jerky, almost bounding way of walking. The girl in white ceased her laughter, sat rigidly in her chair. D'Enry's head twisted about and every person at that gay table seemed turned suddenly to stone.

Wentworth leaned toward Nita, whispering. "The man crossing the floor, isn't that Scott Haillie?" he asked. "I thought he was with the embassy in France."

"He came in yesterday," Nita replied. "I saw his name in the papers."

Scott Haillie had reached the group now. D'Enry was on his feet and the other two men were rising. Wentworth was struck at once with the extreme dignity of the man at the head of the table, tall and haughty-shouldered, his face made commanding by a thin imperious nose, a black-pointed beard.

The third man stepped from the table and confronted Haillie. There was an angry tension in the posture of both. Wentworth smiled at Nita.

"As a friend of Haillie," he murmured, "I think I am called on to intervene. What do you think?"

Nita's tinkling laughter followed him as he strode swiftly

across the floor. This was an excellent opportunity, made to order, for him to form a direct contact with D'Enry and his distinguished-seeming associates. As Wentworth advanced, he studied the group at the table. The headwaiter already had appeared in the background, his solicitous hands making small soothing gestures. The girl in white sat rigidly.

Wentworth's glance at the smooth olive oval of her face was a tribute. Her features were delicate beneath the smooth sweep of night-black hair drawn softly back from a center part and knotted loosely at the nape. Her neck was slender, her dress simple and white, with a conservative décolletage that only hinted at the warm beauty of her shoulders and breasts. Her great black eyes were frightened as they stared fixedly at the face of Scott Haillie.

Next to her stood D'Enry, drawn to his full brief height, small bright eyes challenging beneath the sharp line of his brows. The other woman beside him seemed bewildered by the abrupt hostility about her. Obviously, she was the mother of the girl, though her face, a blurred echo of her daughter's, lacked the younger's fine-drawn intelligence.

WENTWORTH'S EYES went next to the bearded man, the father. Closer scrutiny confirmed the earlier impression of kingliness. There was a black imperiousness about his eyes, arrogance in the dark flush that had spread to high cheekbones. He was easily an inch taller than Wentworth's six feet and as he placed a hand upon the back of his chair to set it aside, Wentworth saw the rich gleam of a gold signet-ring that bore a coat of arms.

These things the Spider took in with a single sweeping glance as he stepped to Haillie's side. The man who faced the Spider's friend was obviously the son of the bearded one, brother of that lovely girl. The young man's face, dark with anger, had his father's imperious eyes and the fierce lights in their depths.

"You have been told," he said with a harsh accent, "that your presence is not desired. Have the courtesy to retire."

"May I be of any service?" Wentworth interrupted quietly. "Mr. Haillie is my friend."

Scott Haillie jerked his head about. Wentworth saw the sparkle of anger in the sharp blue eyes, but the face was expressionless, as unruffled as his sleekly blond hair.

"Yes," said Haillie in a low voice that trembled slightly. "Yes," he repeated. "You can pluck this infant from my path so that I may have an intelligent word with his father."

The blood ebbed from the face of the dark youth. He stepped in close; his right hand flew out. The open palm smacked loudly against Haillie's left cheek!

At the blow, a small smothered cry jerked from the girl. It was startlingly loud and Wentworth realized that every other sound in the room was muted. The strumming of music had ceased. The constant, noisy concatenation of talking was stilled.

"André," the father's voice rang with harsh imperiousness, "André, you will apologize. This must go no farther."

Haillie had not wavered at the heavy blow. His back became more rigid, his blond head lifted higher. At the elder man's words, his lips twitched slightly. He turned toward Wentworth, drew out a card-case with hands that were completely steady.

"Will you inquire of the gentlemen," he requested flatly, "to whom I may present my card?"

Wentworth was frowning. "Don't be ridiculous, Haillie," he said in a swift undertone. "Duels are not fought in America these days."

He knew even before he spoke that the words were futile. It was ridiculous, positively fantastic, this scene upon the roof of a New York hotel. It might have been Paris of a hundred years ago—an angry man demanding that death pay for a blow. Haillie's bitter eye burned into his. Wentworth stepped back, bowed, and turned toward the youth.

"Permit me," he said. "I am Richard Wentworth. My principal..." he hesitated.

"André," the father repeated harshly. "This must go no farther."

André slowly folded his arms. He seemed to gain an inch in height, and a smile as faint, as cold as that which had touched Haillie's lips disturbed his own.

"D'Enry," he said without raising his voice. "This gentleman is Richard Wentworth. He has a card he wishes to present. *M'sieur*, this is my friend and second, Remarque D'Enry."

Wentworth turned with veiled eyes. This was the moment for which he had been waiting—the reason for his intervention in this matter—to meet D'Enry face to face. Now his purpose was widened. He must investigate these people with whom the revolutionist was on such intimate terms. It was possible they had some connection with the operations of the pirate band? A slightly mocking smile crossed Wentworth's lips as he bowed again. Who but the Spider would dream of suspecting such eminently respectable persons?

The Frenchman stepped back from the two ladies with a murmur of apology. Wentworth noted just before the man greeted him that the girl's eyes still were fixed on Haillie's face; she held her handkerchief pressed to her lips. Strangely, though, there was a tinge of admiration in those black staring eyes.

D'Enry's gaze met Wentworth's mockingly. The Frenchman was clean-shaven save for a thin black mustache that jutted its spiked ends horizontally above the mocking curve of his lips.

"M'sieur?" murmured D'Enry.

Wentworth felt, rather than heard, the approach of the father. D'Enry swung about, clicking his heels.

"Señor Don Estéban de Cinquado y Janández," he murmured, *"M'sieur* Richard Wentworth who presents the card of *M'sieur* Scott Haillie."

WENTWORTH MET the father's imperious eyes. There was a genuineness about this man, but there was ruthlessness, too. Could this man be involved in D'Enry's plans? Could this be the intelligence that directed the skillful, merciless blows of the Pirates?

For the first time since he had entered this warfare with the killers, Wentworth felt that he had met a man who could have formulated such a conspiracy. He did not believe a man with that thin-lipped, imperious mouth, with those burning eyes would hesitate to kill thousands to achieve his ends. The man was a supreme egotist, cast in the mold of the ancient emperors. But none of Wentworth's thoughts showed on his face. He met Don Estéban's gaze inquiringly.

"Will you gentlemen have the kindness to accompany me to my rooms?" Don Estéban requested in a tone that was more like a command than an invitation.

Wentworth assented, arranged for Haillie to take Nita to the Spider's apartment, there to await the results of the conference. When he returned, the two de Cinquado women were already threading a way through the tables, the girl with her head held high and arrogantly. The four men followed and it was two hours before Wentworth returned to his apartment.

"The weapons are rapiers," Wentworth reported to Haillie. "The time, daybreak; the place, the Dueling Rocks across the river."

"Splendid!" Haillie exclaimed with a bleak smile. "If I can contrive it, I'll spill his blood in exactly the same spot that Aaron Burr did such a neat job on Alexander Hamilton."

Wentworth stared speculatively at the man. He was accepting this bizarre arrangement as the most ordinary thing in the world. Imagine a duel in America in the twentieth century, fought with swords on the famous dueling ground of by-gone days! Wentworth himself had fought with swords more than once, but his was a life of adventure and strange battles. This man was presumably a staid diplomat—yet he deliberately entered into a duel.

There was a serious side of the matter also. If the duel resulted fatally, all participants, seconds as well as principals, faced a death penalty as accessories. The prospect entertained Wentworth, but there was more than that involved. He hoped, through the medium of the duel, to learn more about D'Enry and to discover the relations between him and the dignified Latin.

On his way home from the Don's apartment, Wentworth had called a newspaper friend of his to inquire about the man.

"Don Estéban!" the newspaper man had cried. "Do I know him? Say, my back sides still ache from the time his peons tossed me out. Say, listen, he's America's only king. Fact!"

Don Estéban, it developed, had held a huge *hacienda*, high in the mountains in almost feudal style, ruling the peons in life and death. Driven out by the same mounting federal power that had expelled Miguel Oriano and his whip from Mexico, the *hidalgo* had contracted to buy an island off the coast of Yucatan where he would have complete and independent sovereignty. Since that time, he had established an island kingdom of rare beauty. And he was incredibly strong as marauding *banditos* had learned to their cost when they had made an attempt at the millions Don Estéban was reputed to have.

What, Wentworth wondered, could be the history of Haillie's entanglement with this American king? It was abruptly clear to the Spider that such an island kingdom, free from supervision by external officials and by representatives of other governments, *would* be a perfect headquarters for the operation of the pirate band. Those planes he had destroyed had come out of the south, where the island lay!

Haillie got slowly to his feet, glancing at his watch. "Thanks a lot, Dick," he said. "I'd better be turning in. I don't want to be late. You'll call for me?"

Wentworth nodded slowly, eyes intent on the angular strength of Haillie's face. Haillie was, perhaps, a year or two younger than Wentworth, a stockier, broad-shouldered man. His face in repose had a harsh power emphasized by the mockery that played now about his lips.

Haillie came of prodigally wealthy people, and had been reared with the expectancy of great inherited riches. Brilliant, but mentally indolent, he had preferred to idle his way through school, but he had done it in a wholly charming way that had disarmed his instructors and made him an idol of the under-graduates. A few sports had interested him. He had been a bounding demon on the tennis court, with a powerful slashing game that had driven many a technically better player to despair. He had displayed the same furious energy in fencing classes and on the polo-field.

In later years a series of misfortunes had wiped out his family's money. Influence had placed him in the diplomatic service. It had been five years since Wentworth had seen him. During the interim, Haillie had held a half-dozen posts, usually in Paris, and had acquired a suave polish that the bounding malingerer of college days would have mocked in another.

Wentworth was jerked from the preoccupation of his thoughts by Nita's soft voice. "I know it's most impolitic, Scott," she said, "but do tell me something about that charming girl we saw tonight. I'm sure this whole affair dates back to some moonlit night in the *Bois du Boulogne....*"

Haillie smiled gravely. His voice when he spoke was as light as Nita's. "It was in Seville, to be precise, on a hot mid-after-noon," he told her, "and at a *corrida de toros*, a bull-fight, not the *Bois*. I was struck by her appetite for blood. She actually licked her lips every time *picador* or *banderillero* struck and she rather seemed to like the little affair of the horses."

Nita matched his banter. "Then by all means, you must give her the opportunity of watching your little *corrida* in the morning," she said. Wentworth broke in to remind Haillie that he must sleep.

What, actually, Nita had sought to learn was the reason behind the duel, but that Wentworth thought he already knew. He had learned at the home of Don Estéban that Haillie had met the girl abroad and had made a wildly youthful play to win her. At first she had favored him, then dropped him abruptly— apparently at the insistence of her father. The gleam in the girl's eyes at the night club, plus what Haillie now said of the *corrida de toros*, told him the story. Haillie was playing a subtle game, apparently still determined to win the girl. He knew that the romantic appeal of the duel, the startling elements of such an action in America, would pull the girl strongly to him.

Wentworth explained these things rapidly to Nita when Haillie had gone, but before he could skim through more than half the history. Ram Singh strode silently into the room, his bare feet soundless on the waxed floors, his white house garments throwing his sharp, hawk-like features into strong relief. Arms folded, he stood quietly until Wentworth turned toward him, realizing that his faithful Hindu had something to communicate. Ram Singh executed a smooth salaam, spoke in precise, stiff English.

"*Sahib,*" he said, "I have that to report which should not have to be said. When I first found this Remarque D'Enry, it was half by accident, and I was not in disguise. Tonight when I returned to the domicile of my master, two men followed me."

Wentworth frowned suddenly. "And these two?" he asked.

"I have them in the blue guest-room, *sahib.*" Ram Singh bowed again.

"Are they in a condition to be questioned?" Wentworth asked quietly, and a small smile touched his lips at his servant's way of informing him of the capture.

Ram Singh's face was entirely grave.

"Within a half hour, *sahib,*" he said "I will have them conscious."

He cupped his hands to his forehead and backed smoothly from the room. Wentworth turned to Nita. She was laughing softly, her head of chestnut curls gleaming with bronze lights beneath a low-shaded lamp.

"Ram Singh is inimitable," she said. "I was worried for a moment."

Wentworth dropped to the davenport beside her, gazed off into the shadows that obscured the farther side of the richly-garnished room. Perhaps from these two prisoners he might learn something of value. If they were Mexicans it would indicate a close tie-up between D'Enry and Don Estéban. Dimly, he heard the buzz of the door bell, saw the silent passage of his old butler Jenkyns.

Suddenly, without warning, a strangled cry rang out in the hallway. Wentworth jerked to his feet, snapped a hand to the gun beneath his arm. He sprang aside from Nita in the same movement, then froze without drawing the weapon. A man in the doorway held a sub-machine gun cuddled on his right hip. A handkerchief was tied over the lower half of his face.

"Take it easy, boy friend," the man growled, "or I'm going to turn you into a nasty spot on that pretty rug of yours."

CHAPTER 6
TREACHERY!

WHILE HE spoke, three more men showed behind him in the shadows of the hall. All carried automatic pistols and one dangled a blackjack from his wrist. Wentworth's mouth tightened. He knew the aged Jenkyns had felt the weight of that sap.

"Nita," Wentworth called, "Listen closely!" He spat out a few words in French, lapsed into Hindustani, rasping it all in a penetrating voice.

The man with the machine gun shook his head slowly.

"That ain't going to do you a bit of good, boy friend," he said "Jim, keep a rod on the dame. He's talking funny talk to her."

He had not taken his eyes off Wentworth. "Now, listen, we ain't planning to hurt anybody, but two buddies of mine followed a fellow into your place and they ain't come out again. I want 'em!"

A swift frown crossed Wentworth's face. Evidently the two who had followed Ram Singh had been in turn followed by others. It was clever shadowing. Evidently, too, they were not

Mexicans. That fact did not clear Don Estéban of suspicion, but at least it did not involve him. It was obvious that D'Enry had formed an alliance with American gangsters. Good Lord! Were these the men behind the plans for revolution?

Wentworth smothered a curse. If any of these men got back to the leader from whom they came, Wentworth would be linked with the affair of the pirates. They would not, of course, have any indication that he was the Spider, but that in itself would make no difference. The mere fact that he was known as their enemy would hinder his work.

Abruptly the lights winked out in the room—flashed out in the hall where the four gunmen stood. Wentworth flung himself aside, glimpsed swift movement as Nita sprung behind the davenport as he had told her to do in French at the same time he had ordered Ram Singh in Hindustani to do tricks with the lights.

As Wentworth hit the floor, jerking out his automatic, he saw the glitter of Ram Singh's throwing knife streaking from darkness into light, and the machine-gunner's head flew back. His hands, dropping the heavy weapon, groped toward the knife-hilt that protruded from his throat.

Wentworth's automatic was barking now. His bullets caught one of the men in the hall. The other two jumped to cover even as their companions crumpled to the floor. Once more a knife glinted, flying across the hall and a gurgling scream rang through the apartment. An instant later, the door clapped shut.

"Follow him, Ram Singh," Wentworth called.

The white-clad Hindu flitted down the hall and Wentworth

got deliberately to his feet. He fixed the lights, tossed a sheet over the bodies in the doorway before he called Nita from her hiding place behind the davenport. She was pale but composed and sat silently smoking while Wentworth searched the bodies. There was absolutely nothing to identify them or give a clue to their leader. By the time he had finished, police had arrived, and only because the officers knew in what esteem Wentworth was held by the Commissioner of Police, Stanley Kirkpatrick, did they accept his calm assertion that he knew of no reason for the attack.

When finally, they had gone, Wentworth went to the blue guest-room where Ram Singh had put the two prisoners. He stopped at the entrance, staring. On twin beds where they had been tied, lay slashed remnants of their bonds, but the men themselves were gone!

Wentworth stared down at the pieces of manila and his lips tightened ominously. It was certain that the men had been prisoners at the time Ram Singh had told of their capture. It followed that the two must have escaped while police were in the house. And that meant Ram Singh would be caught between the man he was following and the two who had escaped!

Swiftly Wentworth sought to trace the Hindu to warn him of his predicament, but the faithful Ram Singh had vanished without a trace. As the long hours of the night dragged by, the Spider's worst fears were confirmed. It was their invariable rule for Ram Singh to communicate at intervals when separated on a case, and throughout the night the Hindu had not called. WHEN THE false dawn showed grayly above the eastern terrace of Wentworth's apartment, he sent Nita home by taxi, prepared to go to the Dueling Rocks with Haillie. Ram Singh's disappearance was a severe blow, but he must carry on. Before this, his companions, even his loved ones had fallen into the enemy's hands. Always he had pushed on to the battle. Even though Ram Singh's life was held forfeit for his dropping the case, Wentworth would have persisted. The Spider and his colleagues must come second to the needs of humanity, the good of the people and the country must override any personal sacrifice.

So Wentworth prepared to push on with his plans for closer acquaintance with Don Estéban, trying to fathom the secret behind the association of the revolutionist D'Enry with America's only king. But he was wan of face and grave as his chauffeur, Jackson, drove him through the dark deserted streets to Scott Haillie's hotel, then to the North river dock where one of Wentworth's smaller motor cruisers was moored. Just before they shoved off, Wentworth led Jackson aside and spoke swiftly to him. Jackson nodded gravely, strode away. Wentworth dropped to the boat where Haillie already waited. A chill wind swept in off the Hudson, but the motor caught at the first touch of the starter button and Wentworth slid the motor into gear.

"The others bringing the surgeon?" Haillie asked.

Wentworth turned his grimly smiling face to the other.

"We decided we couldn't trust a doctor," he said "You'll have to depend on my humble services."

Haillie shrugged. He seemed utterly calm, his face expressionless.

Nevertheless, as Wentworth split the breeze-ruffled waters, he felt an indefinable sense of impending peril. The thought of Ram Singh's disappearance rankled. It was very likely that D'Enry knew of Wentworth's espionage by now, probable that he would prepare some trap.

With a start, Wentworth realized that this entire affair—the quarrel and the duel—might have been arranged by D'Enry. At least, the Frenchman had done nothing to pacify the two antagonists. His attitude during the conferences had been belligerently insistent. Wentworth wondered if Haillie, too, were slated for elimination by the wily revolutionist and his allies. Perhaps Haillie had learned something about the Frenchman, perhaps he knew of some alliance between D'Enry and the Don.

"If I'm not being too personal," Wentworth said to Haillie, "what is the fight all about anyway?"

Haillie shrugged. "You probably know the history of my little affair abroad with Carmencita. When the family left the country, I followed here. D'Enry, a disreputable little rat from the Montmartre, for whom I once did a favor, phoned me that they were staying at the *St. Delroy* and dining in public. I jumped at the chance. André interfered and my temper got the best of me—"

Wentworth smiled slightly, nodding.

"It's not the first time a man has risked his life for a girl," he said absently. His mind was racing. This confirmed his subconscious fears that D'Enry was behind the entire thing! But what secret could Haillie hold that would cause the Frenchman to seek his destruction? The man would know that murdering

Haillie, a diplomat, would cause a furor. But if he could maneuver it so that the diplomat was killed in a duel over a girl….

The black irregular rocks of the dueling place showed like worn witch's teeth ahead. Wentworth cut the motor of the boat, allowed it to drift in with diminishing headway. Another similar launch already was beached on a narrow strip of sand and Wentworth guided his own craft steadily, in beside it.

He could not help but think there was something a little mad about this entire affair. Here they were in twentieth-century America preparing to duel at daybreak with rapiers. It had been over a century since Aaron Bum and Alexander Hamilton had come to this spot. Wentworth had a brief mental picture of that chill morning long ago when slaves rowed their masters here to duel with their long-barreled pistols. They came with swords now, in motor-launches, and the field of honor no longer was honorable in the eyes of the law….

WENTWORTH SPRANG ashore without a word, the long sword-case under his arm, and Scott Haillie leaped down beside him nimbly. Together they stalked through the chill early morning up a short rise to the level stretch of ground that from time immemorial had served the gentlemen of New York for settling their disputes of honor.

André and D'Enry were already waiting. The Frenchman hurried forward, his small dark face completely serious for once. As they made final arrangements, Wentworth watched him intently. The man's eyes were withdrawn and secretive, but they gave no clue of what impended. The Spider's feeling of apprehension increased.

They separated to consult their principals and Wentworth swung a searching glance over the scene. It was still only half light, gray dawn silvering the waters of the Hudson. To shoreward, a hill climbed steeply, studded with stones, covered with bushy short growth. The small waves of the faint sunrise wind gurgled and sucked among the black rocks below, and a few sea-gulls wheeled near with faint questioning mews. There were no other sounds.

He felt a strange detachment from all that was about to occur here. There was a spirit of unreality that even the Spider for all his dealings with fabulous plottings found difficult to penetrate. Across the Hudson reared the towers of mighty skyscrapers. A few early ferries tooted hoarsely and here men faced each other with swords on the Dueling Rocks. Behind their meeting loomed an even more fantastic thing, the grinning skull-and-cross-bones flag of piracy!

Wentworth studied the men again. André de Cinquado y Janández, stripped now to trousers and white shirt, light shoes upon his feet, stood with arms folded, staring straight out over the gleaming waters with unseeing eyes, the breeze ruffling his crisp hair. D'Enry was talking at him rapidly now. Haillie was coolly surveying his opponent, his strong straight-mouthed face expressionless. A diamond ring gleamed on his right hand. Wentworth crossed to suggest that he remove it since its flash would mark too plainly the movements of his hand. Haillie refused with a brief negative shake of his head. D'Enry stepped back to one side, a rapier in his hand.

"Ready," he called.

Wentworth caught Haillie's brief nod, and drew a rapier himself.

"Ready," he agreed.

The rapiers which D'Enry and he carried were part of the agreement. Inasmuch as there were to be no other witnesses, no surgeon, no referee, these two with their swords would be the arbiters. Either could break into the duel if he considered unfair tactics were being employed.

"*Salut!*" D'Enry called, then immediately, "*En garde!*"

The swords of the two duelists circled, glinting in the dull light. As the two men glided toward each other with extended blades, left arms at balance behind and over their heads, the first edge of the sun pushed above the horizon and red rays glinted like strange fire along the keen gleaming swords.

Suddenly, without warning, a great crashing of shrubbery sounded on the hillside. A rock, dislodged, came bounding down.

Wentworth flicked a single glance, saw two men struggling upon a narrow ledge, saw that one was his chauffeur, Jackson. Wentworth's rapier flicked out and struck up the blades of the duelists.

"Halt!" he ordered tensely.

HAILLIE SNARLED a curse; André ripped out blistering Spanish, but Wentworth's blade was firm. D'Enry, to one side, was glancing swiftly from the battle on the ledge to the engagement of three swords. He, himself, had made no move to interfere.

"Wait," Wentworth insisted. "We must learn the cause of this interruption. The distraction might prove unfair to my principal."

André and Haillie relaxed their tense poses, drew backward, step by step, but still they did not glance upward at the battlers on the ledge. The two men separated, and Wentworth whirled to peer upward where the red sun gilded the steep black rocks. Jackson's deep-chested body was easy to distinguish. He stood on braced feet, back toward the edge of the narrow ledge, flinging rights and lefts at another man who rushed him, tried to topple him down the slope.

A sharp cry ripped from Wentworth. He caught the gleam of a knife in the hand of the attacker, saw the man come in low with the blade sweeping upward from the ground toward Jackson's belly. But Jackson knew that kind of attack, too. He had been Wentworth's sergeant during the war, a stocky, broad-shouldered hellion with the fiery spirit of Gascón forebears. He had been a man without discipline, the bully of his company as a private and considered an incorrigible until he had come under Wentworth's firm hand. After that the man's rise had been rapid, but he had refused a commission to continue to serve under Wentworth, a major by this time. Yes, he knew how to meet that attack.

Jackson's left arm swept down to one side, knocking the knife clear of his body. His right knee doubled toward his assailant's body and his heavy foot shot forward in a *savate* kick that caught his assailant in the lower abdomen, sprawled him on the rocks. Jackson picked the man up, tossed him over his shoulder, came down the hill with a rifle a-swing in his free hand.

Wentworth jerked his eyes from the descending man to glance at the three with him upon the ledge. Haillie was staring with frowning, puzzled brows. D'Enry's glittering eyes were aflame with rage! André's face was expressionless. The point of his rapier rested upon the toe of his shoe and he waited, staring impassively as before, out over the water.

As Jackson came nearer, bearing his burden lightly on broad shoulders, Wentworth saw that the muzzle of the rifle was covered by an extension of the barrel that was larger in diameter. The rifle had a silencer! He glanced quickly to his man's broad-jawed face and saw that, contrary to custom, it was completely serious. Jackson marched straight up to Wentworth and dumped his burden heavily to the ground. The man writhed, his face contorted with agony. Jackson stood at attention, the gun grounded army style at his right side.

"Following the major's orders, sir," Jackson reported. "I engaged another boat and landed above the dueling rocks, climbed the cliff and came down the edge, keeping a weather-eye open. Upon reaching a spot directly above the rocks, I noticed this man lying in ambush upon a ledge and behind a clump of shrubbery. He had a rifle with a silencer and when I reached the ledge apparently had drawn a bead on this gentleman here…" he nodded toward André.

André started from his stony silence, whirled and stared down at the man, whose writhings were growing quieter. He glanced from him to Haillie and fury blazed in his eyes. His rapier was held free and Wentworth saw by the quiver of the blade that his hand was trembling. He watched alertly as he signed Jackson to go on.

"I jumped him and took him captive, sir," Jackson continued.

"Don't move," D'Enry's voice snapped brittlely, "I have you all covered!"

Wentworth glanced unconcernedly toward the Frenchman, saw that he held a slender-barreled automatic in his right hand, that anger had darkened his face with congested blood.

"André," D'Enry went on, cold-voiced. "It is your privilege to run both these men through. They plotted to murder you upon the field of honor!"

ANDRE'S HAND tightened upon the hilt of his rapier. Haillie threw himself in an attitude of defense, blade alertly before him.

"Just a minute," he said incisively. "I know nothing of this attack. I swear it. Before you jump at conclusions, it might be wise to question this assassin."

Wentworth was studying the three members of the dueling party warily. Jackson had said the man had apparently drawn a bead on André's back. He would have to be very confident of that before he would make such a statement. Therefore, he could not doubt that the assassin had intended to murder the Don's son. But who could have planned the action? Surely not Haillie, for nothing could come out of it for himself except a charge of murder. Could André himself have planned it, intending to betray the man at the last minute in some way and so save himself from the duel?

But André had precipitated the duel himself. How about

Don Estéban, then? Perhaps, desiring to save his son's life, he had intended to have this man wound André and incapacitate him…Wentworth's eyes swept to D'Enry, detected the faintest of smiles upon the lips beneath the spiked mustache. He was instantly sure that D'Enry was involved in the treachery. But why? And how was this fiasco connected with the piracy and revolution which threatened the country?

"I add my assurances to those of Mr. Haillie," Wentworth said calmly. "I think we would do well to question the man."

He turned toward the prisoner, now almost recovered from Jackson's shrewd blow, but still white-faced with pain, his forehead beaded with sweat. He winced as Jackson, seeing Wentworth's nod, turned toward him abruptly and stirred him with his toe.

"Who gave you orders to come here?" Jackson demanded. His voice was harsh, and the man winced again.

He looked up into the faces of the other men about him, but found no mercy in any of them. He looked back to Jackson, cringed. "Nobody," he whined finally.

"What!" Jackson bellowed. He snatched the man by the hair, yanked him to his feet. "What did you say?"

"No, no!" the man whimpered. "Don't hit me again. I lied. I'll talk."

"You'd better," growled Jackson. "Speak up. Who hired you to come here to shoot this gentleman?"

Once more the craven's pain-whitened face, whiter because of the ragged mop of black hair that straggled across his brow, turned slowly to each one of the men. When his eyes reached

Wentworth, he jerked them quickly back to Jackson. "If I tell, you won't let him hurt me?" he begged.

Jackson nodded firmly. Alarm bells were ringing in Wentworth's mind. He knew instinctively that some treachery was afoot here. D'Enry's scarcely hidden glee, the man's recurrent glances at himself. He glanced toward the Frenchman and found that the venomous automatic was centered upon himself.

"Be sure," Wentworth spoke gravely to the assassin, "that you tell the truth."

The man jerked his head in a frightened nod. *"You* want me to tell the truth?" he asked humbly.

Wentworth's eyes narrowed. He took his rapier in both hands, the left near the tip of the blade, "I order you to tell the truth, and nothing but the truth," he snapped.

"Okay," the man's tone was resigned. "I was ordered to come here and hide up in the rocks," he twisted his neck and stared up toward the spot where he and Jackson had fought, "and to drop two men. You—" a nod toward André, "and you." A nod toward D'Enry.

"Who gave you those orders?" Haillie snapped, his face lowering with menace.

The man's frightened eyes swung to Wentworth. He raised a hand that trembled and pointed it. "The man who told me to kill them," he said, "is *Mr. Wentworth!*"

CHAPTER 7
DEATH ON THE ROCKS

WENTWORTH STARED at the assassin in amazement. He had half suspected some villainy against himself, but this form of attack was totally unexpected. But Jackson acted first. He slapped the man across the mouth. "You lie!" the ex-sergeant roared.

He caught the assassin by the shoulders and shook him violently. "You lie!" he shouted again.

Wentworth let his sword dangle from his left hand, held by the tip alone as he touched Jackson on the shoulder.

"We'll get the truth out of him," he said calmly, turned to face the other three men. "There is a deep-lying plot back of this. Someone is deliberately trying to discredit and involve me. My Hindu boy was captured last night after four gunmen forced their way into my apartment. I am convinced that this is more of the activities of a criminal group whose identity I am not privileged to reveal."

D'Enry's mouth twisted in a sneer. He still held the automatic ready. "And I suppose it will serve your enemy's purpose excellently if my principal and I are killed?"

Wentworth studied the man calmly, trying to fathom the purpose behind his activities. Could this man be the leader of the pirates and revolutionists? He jerked his head in an unconscious negative. No, the leader of so great an enterprise would never expose himself openly in this way to criminal charges. Furthermore, though D'Enry had a quick mind, was clever at detail work, he did not believe the man had the mentality to conceive and organize so vast an enterprise as was evident in this latest conspiracy against humanity.

"You're not questioning my word, *M'sieur* D'Enry?" Wentworth asked. It was spoken quietly, without bravado, but there was a steely challenge in Wentworth's gray-blue eyes.

For an instant the gaze of the two men locked and Wentworth saw caution film the angry gleam of the Frenchman's eyes. D'Enry hesitated.

"If *M'sieur* swears upon his word of honor," he amended reluctantly, "I have no choice but to accept his statement, of course, or meet him at once. *M'sieur* has a certain reputation with the rapier." He shrugged, but despite his words, the automatic still kept its bead on Wentworth's chest. "I am not a coward, but I have the—shall we say—discretion?"

"You are calling me a liar, I believe," said Wentworth, still calmly. His quietness was dangerous. He was weighing the chances. If he killed D'Enry now, would it hamper or help his search for the pirate leader? Although he suspected Don Estéban was involved, D'Enry was the only person he actually knew to be a pirate.

Haillie broke in abruptly. "Come, this has gone far enough. I, for one, accept the word of a gentleman. There is more villainy afoot here than meets the eye. But the plot has failed, and we still have a little argument to settle."

André spoke for the first time then, his voice quivering with suppressed anger. "I do not cross blades with an assassin," he said.

"You will give me satisfaction," Haillie retorted grimly, "or I shall give myself the pleasure of shooting you on sight."

André stiffened. "That would be entirely in keeping with your tactics to date," he said vehemently and tossed his rapier to the ground. "Go ahead. Run me through, dog!"

Haillie's face was dead white. His eyes seemed on fire. He took a half step forward, rapier poised.

"No, Haillie," Wentworth said sharply. "There will come another time of reckoning. Do not soil your blade."

"It would not be wise," D'Enry declared. "In fact, I must ask you to drop your sword, *M'sieur* Haillie. We are, all of us, going to pay a little visit to the police. I think they will be interested in the story of this gentleman we have captured."

"It's absurd," Wentworth burst out. "Why should I plant a man to commit murder, then send another man to stop it?"

D'ENRY SHRUGGED, a hateful smile on his small dark face. "Perhaps you wished an interruption, to save your principal. Perhaps you primed the wretch with some other story and he misunderstood what you meant by ordering him to tell the truth." He shrugged jerkily. "Who am I to read the workings of the criminal mind?"

Wentworth smiled faintly at the words. He still held his sword grasped by the tip, figuring rightly that D'Enry would not consider it a weapon when held in that position, would not force him to drop it. He studied the Frenchman, still weighing his death. If D'Enry had plotted to kill the son of Don Estéban, it was unlikely the two were allies. That meant this man was his sole clue to the identity of the leaders. Learning that was far more important than the destruction of any single cog, no matter of how great importance. No, he could not kill D'Enry.

But neither could he permit the man to hand them to the police. Even if nothing came of the charges, it would delay him with futile inquiries and procedure. They were on the New Jersey side of the Hudson and while the influence of his friend, Stanley Kirkpatrick, Commissioner of New York Police, could extend there, it would not suffice to prevent delay. And days were precious now. He could not doubt that the pirates were planning new forays, that they were perfecting their plot to overthrow the United States.

He glanced from the corners of his eyes at Jackson, saw that the broad shoulders were hunched for action, that beefy hand ready on the rifle. He would stand no chance, though, against that ready automatic.

Wentworth's faint smile faded. He drew back his left hand, grasping the rapier by the tip. "No, Jackson!" he said sharply.

As Wentworth had anticipated, D'Enry jerked eyes and gun toward Jackson, cried a sharp warning. Wentworth bent his wrist backward, tensing the steel blade like a spring, then flipped it forward, moving his arm from the elbow only. The glitter of steel caught D'Enry's eyes. He barked a muffled cry, swung his gun back. Wentworth flung himself to the side and the rapier, sailing true and swiftly, smacked its heavy hilt between the Frenchman's eyes. His bullet chipped the rocks underfoot. He reeled backward and before he could fire again, Jackson was upon him.

Instantly, Wentworth wrenched the gun free, swung to cover his foes. André stood, staring wide-eyed. Haillie was frowning in disapproval, but the wretched man who had lurked in the shrubbery with the rifle had taken advantage of the scuffle to run. Even as Wentworth snatched the gun, the man reached the edge of the rocks and launched himself outward in a dive.

"After him, Jackson," Wentworth snapped. Jackson crossed the level rock like an arrow loosed from its bow, but reaching the verge, he threw himself back on his heels, sprawled down and barely saved himself from a plunge over the edge. He got up then, stared at the water, came back slowly.

"There are rocks just below the surface," he said grimly. "The prisoner hit one with his head."

Wentworth nodded slowly twice. D'Enry was sputtering curses, a hand pressed to his forehead where the rapier hilt had caught him. Abruptly he began to throw his arms about and caper like a man gone mad. He shouted shrilly.

"Stop that!" Wentworth ordered sharply, "or I'll put a bullet through your leg. Jackson, what…."

"Shoot and be damned to you! Son of a pig!" D'Enry shrilled. "Your punishment will be swift and sure."

Wentworth leveled the automatic.

Jackson's voice broke in quietly on the raving. "There's a police launch about a hundred yards off shore, sir," he reported. "They've caught this man's signals and are putting in."

WENTWORTH DID not turn from his wary watch over André and D'Enry. Swift plans raced through his brain. His launch could easily distance the other boat, he knew, but there was no chance to reach it and escape. The police were too close to the shore. Furthermore, the police launch would carry rifles and machine-guns and before he could gain distance his entire craft would be riddled.

No, there was no way of escaping a parley with the police. Even if D'Enry were forced to remain silent, there would be endless questions and delay. The swords scattered about on the rock would be clear enough indication that a duel had been intended. If they happened to see the body in the water or if D'Enry told them of it, there would be more complications.

"Jackson," Wentworth spoke swiftly, "wait until the police are under the brow of the rock, where they can't see us clearly, then gather up the swords and rifle and stow them in a crevice. D'Enry, you must see that nothing is to be gained by revealing the duel. You and Cinquado would be equally to blame and I believe there are some ancient rather stringent, laws which make seconds equally culpable."

D'Enry glared at him without comment. He had ceased his capering now and a mocking smile played about his mouth.

Wentworth turned to André. "You see that, Cinquado?"

The young aristocrat nodded. His crisp black hair had a sheen like a crow's wing.

"Ahoy there on shore!" came the hail from the police boat, "What's going on?"

"We're a fishing party, Jackson," said Wentworth swiftly, eyes still on D'Enry. "We had a little argument and came ashore to settle it with fists. Nothing serious."

Jackson nodded and hurried to the edge of the rocks. D'Enry's smile became a sneer. Jackson's parley from the edge of the rocks was futile. The police declared their intention of coming ashore and Jackson shouted, "Come ahead!"

When the police-boat drew in under the brow of the rocks, he hurriedly gathered up the weapons and hid them. Wentworth tossed his captured automatic over the far brink. He had two guns under his arms, but there was no use in destroying them. He carried permits on those from Kirkpatrick.

Wentworth advanced to meet the police with a smile, but behind the friendliness, his eyes were alert and watchful. Two men were climbing up the path, drawn guns in their hands. Others were close behind them. Wentworth's gaze narrowed. Police boats did not usually carry crews that large. His quick gaze detected signs of furtiveness in the faces of the men. These were not police, he was suddenly positive, but other members of the pirate gang!

The check in Wentworth's advance was scarcely perceptible. He kept on toward the men. Only two had reached the brink, the others still toiled up the steep path. As Wentworth reached the top, he sprang abruptly forward. With a quick shove, he unbalanced the two, sent them reeling toward the edge, guns waving in wild circles over their heads.

"Watch D'Enry!" Wentworth cried over his shoulder.

He charged the false police again, pushed them over, sent them rolling, scrambling down upon the five who climbed the hill below. No answering cry had come from Jackson. Wentworth knew that meant Jackson was out. Without waiting to discover what had happened he threw himself prone upon the edge of the cliff, snatching for his guns rolling to look behind him. But he did not draw. Hands on the butts of his weapons, he paused.

D'Enry stood within ten feet of Wentworth, a second automatic leveled. A glance at the man's eyes told the Spider his death was only seconds away if he made another move. He saw Jackson unconscious on the rocks. D'Enry had apparently struck him down before the cry of warning. Slowly Wentworth took his hands away from his gun butts. He started to get to his feet, but a motion of the Frenchman's automatic kept him prone.

THE SHOUTS and cries of the false police had given way to vile curses which drew nearer. The men had tumbled to the bottom, regained their feet, and were climbing again to the rocks. Jackson was out cold. Haillie and André appeared helpless. There was nothing for it except to lie passively while the Frenchman waited with ready gun and his criminal reinforcements mounted to his assistance.

The scrambling of feet was just behind Wentworth. A man cursed and a kick slammed into his ribs. Wentworth rolled suddenly toward the man, heard a cry of warning. Knees crunched down on his side, but he accomplished his purpose. With a furious screech the man again toppled over the edge, dragging Wentworth with him.

Their plunging bodies struck a rounded rock that jutted out a few feet below the brink, bounced from that into a tangle of shrubbery. As they whirled over in the air, Wentworth caught a brief glimpse of men scattering from their path, saw that only one man remained on the boat but that one pointed a sub-machine-gun toward him.

Wentworth and the man he had knocked from the crest of the ledge were tumbling toward a scrambled pile of water-rounded rocks. Desperately he kicked out with both feet as they brushed the cliff wall. It spun them over, turned the fake policeman underneath just as they landed with a wet, sickening crunch on the rocks. Instantly, Wentworth was on his feet, plunging toward the police-launch. The machine-gun swung toward him. He was twenty feet from the water, but he arched into the air in a headlong dive.

As his body lanced through the air, he curled his head under, landed on his shoulders on the sand in a tumbler's fall. He heard the machine-gun cough into action, heard the wet grating punch of bullets in the sand. He rolled over in a somersault, hit on his feet and dived again. This time he struck the water. Instantly all sound was cut out except the beat of the police-boat engines. The river was icy cold and the chill of it stabbed him to the bone. But Wentworth fought his way deeper and deeper into the frigid flood. That way alone lay hope and life.

Wentworth had hit the water on the far side of his own launch, putting that between him and the supposed police patrol boat. He curved to the left under water and, swimming with powerful full sweeps of his arms, propelled himself under both bottoms. The cold sun came down to him yellowly. The launches were silvery shadows.

Blood pounded in Wentworth's ears. His lungs seemed ready to burst. He must rise to the surface within seconds. Now he had passed under the police boat. With a downward jerk of his hands he shot himself upward, broke water on the far side of the craft where the machine-gunner lurked. He sucked in a great gulp, of air, eyes searching the rocks.

D'Enry was standing on the rim of the path, gun ready in his hand. The other fake policemen were scattered out, eyes scanning the water. Without a ripple, Wentworth re-submerged and swam deep once more, heading for rocks further along the river margin. It was a sixty-foot swim and he barely made the far side of one of the rocks in time. He rested there, panting, teeth chattering with cold. He slipped his automatics from their armpit holsters and held them above the water. They were water-proofed against emergency, but he wanted to make sure they were prepared if it came to a battle.

The odds would be seven-to-one if he were to attack. The Spider had fought against greater odds, but only for vast stakes. It seemed to Wentworth, in water up to his neck, holding the guns carefully above the surface, that this battle would not be worth the risk of death.

Not that he hesitated to brave death himself, but for the sake of the thousands of innocents who would die in piracy and revolution if he should fail.

CHAPTER 8
THE SPIDER FALLS

HE MUST remain in hiding until they tired of the search and left, then he must follow and attempt to smash this foul ring.

For fifteen minutes, while the cold ate to his very bones,

the search for Wentworth was continued, but finally the men trooped to the launch. D'Enry stopped to tumble into the water the body of the man Wentworth had killed in the fall from the rocks, then both the police-boat and André's launch got under way. As they pulled off from shore, there was a sudden brief flurry of action aboard. A man broke free, darted to the side and dived overboard.

Wentworth did not have time to identify him. A machine-gun ripped out. Bullets churned the waters to a froth where he had dived.

Wentworth smothered a groan that chattered out between his teeth. He hoped the man got away, but if the boats hung around to search, if he had to remain in the water another fifteen minutes, he would freeze!

However, the men on the police-boat apparently were satisfied their bullets had finished the fugitive, for the launch pushed on without delaying.

Seconds after the boat had rounded the rocks out of sight, a man's head popped up from the water, a blond head as sleek as a seal. The man was within fifty yards of Wentworth and he swam with hurried, cold-driven strokes toward the shore. The Spider forced himself to remain up to his neck in the freezing water, until the man dragged himself shivering to the shore, until he could see that the fugitive who had escaped the pirate gang was Scott Haillie.

Then Wentworth hallooed Haillie, waded ashore, and running with exaggerated motions to restore the circulation of blood to his blued limbs, led a race to the launch. Haillie wanted to talk, but Wentworth shook his head and got the motor going, the boat under way before he would listen. He motioned Haillie to take the wheel while he ducked into the cabin for dry clothes.

Then, while Wentworth spotted the police launch far up the river and swung in leisurely pursuit, Haillie ducked below to change and told in shouts what had occurred. When the police had taken charge, D'Enry had revealed himself as their leader and declared them all his prisoners. Haillie had managed to escape as Wentworth had seen.

The story brought grim tension to Wentworth's face.

"If D'Enry admitted his position," he said slowly, "it means that André will be killed, along with my man Jackson and two of us—if the criminals can find us."

Haillie, whom Wentworth kept beside him, shook his head ruefully. "It sounds like a chapter out of some penny dreadful magazine," he said. "The old Nick Carter and Dead-Eye Dick stuff we read in the hay-loft as kids."

"It's much worse than that," Wentworth assured him, "worse because everyone regards it just as you say, as purest fiction. Yet I tell you, Haillie, that the nation itself is menaced by the gang with which D'Enry is associated."

Wentworth pointed out then the story of the destruction of the *Remodo* and the bombing of the *America;* cited the possibilities of such modes of attack. Haillie's own face grew grave as he listened—the launch was speeding up the Hudson now—and at the end of the recital, he thrust out his hand, clasped Wentworth's firmly.

"I'm in this thing with you," he declared. "I know that you're

"Au 'voir!" said D'Entry with
a hard laugh as he tumbled
Wentworth over the railing.

fighting it, because it was obvious that the attack on the rocks was aimed especially at you. The kidnaping of your Hindu supports that belief, too."

Wentworth inspected Haillie's firm strong face, his clear blue gaze and nodded slowly. "I promise to use you if I can," he agreed. "For the present, I think we're less apt to arouse suspicion if you get forward and coil a rope or two."

FAR OFF toward the other shore, the supposed police-boat cruised slowly northward, but its green flag had been struck now and glasses showed that the men had doffed uniforms and sat about in white ducks, smoking and chatting. André's boat had disappeared, probably sunk.

Finally the boat turned to a small private wharf on the New Jersey shore at a deserted spot where the shrubbery-shrouded base of the Palisades thrust an almost vertical cliff down into the water. Wentworth made out the small white figures of men walking along a ledge. Jackson and André went with them, arms bound behind their backs, and they entered a rambling cabin, built partly on stilts in the water.

Wentworth spun the wheel then, sent his motorboat creaming the water in a down-river race, for nearly a mile. Then he slanted toward the Jersey shore. It was thirty minutes later that, with idling motor, he edged up to the spot below the wharf where a low spit of land thrust down-stream from the cliff side. The cabin was invisible from this point, hidden behind piled rocks and green growth.

Wentworth's eyes found no lookout, and he stepped ashore. "Your play, Haillie," he whispered, "is to shove off and hold the launch ready either to dart here and pick me up, or to skim by the cabin and snatch me from the water."

Haillie shook his blond head stubbornly. Wet strings of hair sprawled across his brow. "I'll go along," he said. "Give me a gun and we can clean out the whole nest of them."

"There's a gun in the locker at your left," Wentworth told him, "but we can't wipe out the whole lot of them, and escape is going to be the most important item of this raid. It would be a nice feather in your cap if you could save André and take him home to—er—his father."

Haillie hesitated, then nodded slowly. Without another word, Wentworth slipped along a narrow path that slanted upward through thick shrubbery. Cautiously, he crossed the loose rock of a shale slide, reached its peak, and spied down at the cabin. There was a porch which ran along the waterside. A plank walk-way slanted down from a smaller porch on the rear. The one door in sight was closed; the windows were curtained close but thin blue smoke drifted lazily from a tin pipe that jutted through the roof.

There was no way of approach except down the path visible from three windows. Yet, he *must* reach the cabin. D'Enry and at least six of his men were within. André and Jackson were prisoners. It was possible that Ram Singh was held here also, possible that a greater leader than D'Enry was in charge.

With a grimace, Wentworth drew back from the peak of the shale-slide. There was only one other way. He slipped to the shore, spotted his launch pushing slowly against the current fifty yards off shore. He nodded in satisfaction and doffing a heavy jacket, crawled once more into the freezing waters of the Hudson.

Swimming in short laps beneath the surface, he worked his way up to the cabin and ten minutes later was safely beneath the porch. He found a ladder of cleats nailed to one of the pilings and climbed soddenly up it. Once more Wentworth glanced out into the river. His launch was almost directly opposite now, cruising slowly. He cursed as he saw that Haillie was looking intently toward him. Didn't the fool have any sense? If the men in the cabin were at all suspicious, they would spot a man who stared so steadily at their hide-out. But there was no help for it. He could only push on rapidly and hope that Haillie would not be seen.

WENTWORTH CLIMBED the ladder rapidly, peeped over the edge of the porch. A blank wall faced him and he legged over the railing undetected. His lips were blue with cold again. It was with difficulty that he kept his teeth from chattering as the chill bite of the river wind struck him. He pushed on, leaving a wet trail.

With speedy thoroughness, he surveyed the cabin. The porch extended along the river side beneath two windows and a door. On the up-river side there were two windows also. Wentworth dropped to hands and knees, squeezed against the wall, and crawled toward a window. Jubilantly, he saw that it was open a narrow slit. He made out the mutter of voices.

"…with this program," said the quick light tones of D'Enry, "we should be able to accomplish war within six weeks. After that, why should we care what happens to the United States? We shall be rich…."

Wentworth flopped abruptly on his belly, rolled and snatched for the guns beneath his arms. He had caught the soft tread of a foot upon the porch.

As his shoulders hit the boards, Wentworth stared upward into the amazed face of a man who fumbled toward his hip-pocket. Wentworth had his automatics already clear, but instead of firing, he drew back his right hand and hurled the heavy weapon directly into the man's face! At the same instant, Wentworth sprang to his feet. But there was no need of further battle. The gun had caught the man between the eyes. It was necessary only to catch him as he slumped to the deck. The automatic struck the boards with a hollow clatter.

"What's the matter, Hipsy?" called a gruff voice from inside the cabin.

Wentworth whirled around, saw that the door had been left open. He husked out a half dozen ribald curses, swearing at a bucket. He wanted the men inside to think that Hipsy had stumbled over something. He heard coarse laughter and stumped deliberately toward the door, a gun in each hand.

Even as he stalked toward the door, Wentworth's mind was flitting back to the words he had overheard as he crouched beneath the window. D'Enry had spoken of war, had callously hinted once more at the doom of the United States. What in heaven's name could be the plan of the fiends behind this piracy?

His eyes narrow with anger, he whirled into the door. "Hands up, all of you!" he snapped.

The men were sprawled about the room smoking in an attitude of ease, two lying back upon the lower bunks of the four tiers against the far wall. Others slouched in chairs, but D'Enry, alertly poised on his feet, apparently had been pacing up and down the smoke-clouded room behind the rough table in its center. Jackson and André were not in sight.

"Quickly," Wentworth ordered again, and his voice rasped.

Slowly men's hands moved upward. Out of the tail of his eye, Wentworth saw a gangster seated in a rocking-chair slowly twisting his body to cover a draw. The Spider made no attempt to prevent that, only waited until the man's right shoulder jerked with sudden motion, then drilled him between the eyes. The man's head snapped back; his body slumped in the rocking-chair and it teetered slowly backward and forward.

"I really mean it," said Wentworth coolly, his guns weaving hungrily. "Put your hands up, and put them up empty."

D'Enry was cursing in a low, amazed tone. "You're a hard man to kill, Mr. Wentworth," he said softly. "You survive a fall from a cliff that kills another man. You escape both machine-gun bullets and drowning and…."

"Shut up," Wentworth snapped. "You there," he jabbed his left gun toward a fat-faced beefy man, "take that rope in the corner and tie up everyone here. Start with D'Enry."

"You fat pig…!" D'Enry began. A belching shot from Wentworth's right hand gun stopped him. The bullet sang close to the Frenchman's ear.

"Hurry, fat pig," Wentworth mimicked D'Enry, "or I'll

slough some of that fat off of you." The man moved with ludicrous speed, his fat sides shaking.

"Jackson!" Wentworth raised his voice. "Jackson! André!"

A SHARP cry from above answered him, but he did not raise his eyes that way. Apparently there was a shallow attic above the cabin and the two prisoners had been stowed away there. Wentworth continued to point the guns until the gangster had tied everyone, then he proceeded to bind the "fat pig." He glanced out the window at the man he had hit between the eyes, but the fellow was showing no signs of returning consciousness. Blood was seeping from his nostrils.

With a quick nod, Wentworth sprang to a ladder that led upward, freed Jackson and André from their bonds. The Spanish boy was fuming with anger; Jackson was quietly alert.

"On the porch, Jackson," Wentworth ordered swiftly. "Signal Haillie in the launch to come and get André, then you and I are going to ask D'Enry a few questions."

Jackson looked intently into Wentworth's face and a slow grin spread his wide good-humored mouth. There was a hard glint in his eyes. He swung down through the square trap-door into the room below. Wentworth and André followed. Haillie came speedily at their signal, clambered to the porch, and peered inside.

"Good!" he said, and a sudden flush colored his face. "By God, I'd like to whip them all within an inch of their lives. Let's take them to the police."

Wentworth shook his head slowly, smiling at Haillie's rage. "This is my battle you know," he said. "We will call in the police… later. Meantime, you can take André back home. When you return for me, I'll be ready to leave."

Haillie frowned obstinately, stared about at the prostrate men. His eyes lingered longest on D'Enry, He bent over, caught him by the throat with his left hand, smacked his jaws heavily with his right. Wentworth started forward at the first blow, then when he saw Haillie planned no murder, he stopped and let him cuff the Frenchman.

D'Enry squirmed and cursed; presently Haillie straightened. His eyes were queerly bright.

"That did me good," he said, sending breath whistling through his nostrils. "Now, I'll go."

He crossed the room to the porch. André faced him there and without a word, the two men shook hands. Then they went down the ladder. The boat put-putted away. Wentworth turned toward the door, and stopped, jaw locking rigidly. D'Enry stood there with an automatic leveled in his hand!

The gun's muzzle covered Jackson and Wentworth impartially and there was a tight grin on the mouth of the Frenchman. *"M'sieur,"* he said softly, "it pains me deeply…."

Jackson roared out a curse. Wentworth cried a warning, but the brave fellow had already lurched forward in a charge. D'Enry's gun spoke sharply, then wrenched toward Wentworth before he could take advantage of the second's delay. Jackson had been stopped dead in his tracks by the shot. Blood oozed from his head. He wavered backward a step. Wentworth's hands flew out to catch him, but he was too late. Jackson toppled over the railing, struck the water with a sullen splash.

Wentworth ripped off his coat to dive after him. "You fiend," he raged. "He'll drown!"

"Exactly," D'Enry crooned, "but you won't care."

As D'Enry spoke, the automatic spat again. Wentworth felt a numbing shock strike his chest, felt a sudden infinite weakness. He shook his head sharply, staring with widening eyes at the Frenchman. D'Enry had shot him! Wentworth raised a hand slowly to his chest, felt a warm wetness there. Darkness crowded in on his vision. The figure of the Frenchman receded, approached, then faded again. Abruptly Wentworth found himself on the floor, his nails digging into the planks.

He heard words spoken clearly, "That closes your chapter, *M'sieur* Spider." He tried to answer, to shout a denial until, with the abruptness of lightning crashing from the skies, blackness smote and overwhelmed him.

D'Enry crossed to the prostrate Spider, stooped and touched a finger to the throat pulse. The gun was still ready in his right hand. What he felt evidently pleased him. He nodded, holstered his revolver and laboriously hoisted Wentworth's body to the railing.

"Au 'voir," D'Enry said with a hard laugh as he tumbled the body overboard. For a moment it bobbed on the current, then the air went out of the already wet clothing and it sank slowly. Widening ripples lapped among the pilings of the cabin.

D'Enry bunched his fingers, kissed their tips and threw the kiss at the ripples with an expansive gesture. "I did not mean *Au 'voir,"* he said, "I meant *adieu.* The end!"

CHAPTER 9
HAVOC REIGNS

TORTURE WITH hot irons. Nightmares of pain and sinking into bottomless depths. Flashes of unutterable peace that made the hells of agony between unendurable. Gradually those periods of peace lengthened, the gnawing fury of the pain eased and a time came when Wentworth saw the face of Nita, saw that it was wet with tears and knew somehow that they were tears of happiness. That was three weeks after D'Enry had shot him—tumbled him into the freezing waters of the Hudson.

It was three days more before Wentworth could speak above a whisper, five before he could be told what had happened: Jackson's skull had only been creased by the bullet that had tumbled him into the Hudson; the shock of cold water had revived him in time to drag Wentworth, unconscious and bleeding from a wound that pierced his lungs, to the safety of the shore.

Then Jackson had seized D'Enry's fake police launch and raced Wentworth to a hospital. For three weeks, he had lain between life and death, stricken with pneumonia and fever and gunshot wound; but in the end his magnificent strength, his will to live, had triumphed, and he was now definitely on the mend.

Nita told him that D'Enry had not been seen since the day of the shooting, which was true. She told him that there had been no more pirate raids on ships, in saying which she ignored the deaths of seven thousand persons at sea. She said that the country was at peace and that the Spider had broken the back of the pirate strength—and kept to herself the fact that mobs even now howled through the cities of the nation demanding war.

While the Spider had lain, helpless with his wound, the pirates had looted a dozen great ships. Naval vessels, pacing them as guards, had been blown up without warning by planes that swept over them in the darkness. Lifeboats of sailors and marines, still battling to protect the passenger vessels they guarded had been rifled with machine-gun bullets by diving planes; small bombs had blown them into oblivion—and the ships had been stripped and sunk in retribution for daring to protect themselves.

Certain newspapers had carried long articles by war experts saying that only a certain Far Eastern power could be behind the attacks. It was conspicuous that only American ships were sunk. British, French, Scandinavian vessels sailed the seas unscathed. But let an American vessel sally from the protection of the shore and bombs rained from the skies.

Seamen struck, refused to operate ships. Industries within the nation, unable to move their goods, shut down their plants. Thousands of men were thrown out of work and poured into the streets to strengthen the mobs that were demanding action by the government. The navy tried to act, God knew. Its men died trying, but accomplished nothing against the deadly bombs from the sky that struck without warning, crashing through decks, ripping apart the bowels of ships and killing, killing, killing….

When these things failed, the mobs picked up a new cry. They demanded war—war against the nation the experts and the paid men of the pirates blamed for these assaults upon America. Each new attack upon the few ships that braved the seas added fuel to the flames. Rioting was almost continuous in the streets of major cities. This was the situation the day that Wentworth became strong enough to hear how he had been rescued—and was told peace and quiet ruled the country.

Not that Nita was to be blamed. She knew the great spirit of the man she loved, knew his devotion to his country and his people. If he had known the truth, he would have driven his gaunt, fever-weakened body from the bed to his task. Even the Spider could not have survived that. Either his illness would have overpowered him or his weak blows would have aroused the enemy finally to accomplish his death.

There was no doubt they intended to kill him, that they kept never-ending watch on the hospital. For that reason, since Wentworth had been in the hospital, four armed guards had sat constantly outside his door, put there by Stanley Kirkpatrick, commissioner of New York's police. Those policemen who listened in at the hospital switch-board caught telephone calls in which the criminals kept track of his condition, waiting, biding their time to strike. For as long as Wentworth lived D'Enry was foredoomed.

THESE THINGS, too, Wentworth did not know at first, but one fact they could not keep from him and it deepened the dark circles beneath his eyes, tightened his lips in the death's-head that was his face—Ram Singh had vanished. Since the night when he had set out, on Wentworth's order to trail the gunmen who invaded his apartment, the faithful Hindu had

The remaining two gunmen took the full blast of the sawed-off double-barreled shotgun.

not been seen nor heard from. The Spider received that news without change of expression, without a word, but a fire began to glow in his sunken, blue-gray eyes from that moment.

It was the day after he received that news, the first day he was allowed to sit in a wheel-chair and receive visitors, that Scott Haillie, carefully coached by Nita beforehand, came to see Wentworth. He talked cheerfully for five minutes about unimportant affairs, waving his suave hands with the glitter of the large diamond ring that he never took from his finger, his blond hair more sleekly smooth than ever.

"Don Estéban left town the day after our dueling *fiasco*," Haillie said. "I've been looking for D'Enry ever since. I shall kill the rat on sight."

He chided Wentworth gently for sending him away from the cabin the day of the shooting. "If you hadn't done that, D'Enry would already be dead," he growled.

A small twisted smile disturbed Wentworth's lips. "D'Enry is as good as dead," he said, with the low voice of his weakness. "I warn you, Haillie, that if you cheat me of my vengeance, I'll hail you to the Dueling Rocks myself."

Haillie laughed, grasped Wentworth's thin, illness-whitened hand, and left.

It was two hours later that a mob howled its way past the hospital. Wentworth had heard that sound before, had known the madness of rioting thousands upon the streets. He whirled his chair to the window and stared down.

Four stories below him, a band of ragged men and screeching women was filing past. In their forefront a man dragged a flag that Wentworth recognized, the flag of a powerful Eastern nation. A great placard carried by two other men demanded war with that nation. Other placards read:

AVENGE OUR DEAD!
WIPE OUT THE PIRATES!

Wentworth gazed down with tumult pounding in his breast, realized the deception that had been practiced upon him, realized that while he had been ill and convalescent—five weeks in all—the nation had been riven by rioting and war talk, for such things as this did not spring up overnight; he realized that the piracy must have been going on.

There was no blame for Nita in his mind. He knew that she had sought only to build him to strength before she told him the fearful things that were happening; he knew that she was right, but another thing he realized too: unless something intervened at once, the country he loved would be plunged into a disastrous war by which the pirates expected to profit. He smiled grimly. Unless something intervened? He was quibbling with words. What or who could intervene save the Spider?

Should he call in Stanley Kirkpatrick and tell him what he knew? Kirkpatrick would instantly throw all his forces into the battle. But, damn it, the Spider did not know anything! He knew that D'Enry was in the battle, that an infamous revolutionist slaver named Miguel Oriano was one of the pirates. He suspected Don Estéban—and that was all.

Already police were searching for Oriano and D'Enry. They could do no more in that direction. His suspicions of the Don were based solely on the fact that he owned an island which might serve as a pirate rendezvous. Opposed to that was the fact that D'Enry obviously had tried to murder Don Estéban's son. That certainly did not indicate an alliance between the two.

No, there was nothing helpful he could tell Kirkpatrick. He could only throw himself into the battle once more and seek to ferret out the truth—to smash this vile conspiracy from within. And he was weak. He knew that Nita and the doctors would not consent to his leaving the hospital. Wentworth gazed at the mob in the streets, screeching hysterically.

A SMALL man with a hat perched high upon his head turned the corner into the street where the mob crawled. He walked along steadily, head bowed, staring down at the pavement. A group separated from the mob as if it had been ripped loose by an explosion. With a curse, Wentworth realized what was happening. That small man was a national of the country whose flag these mad beasts dragged in the dust!

Even while the oath rasped in his throat, the crowd was upon the man. He stopped, startled, whirled to run. Rocks and cobblestones snatched from the streets bounced about him. Caught in the back of the head by a rock, he flung up his hands and pitched to the earth. The mad pack lunged for the fallen man.

Wentworth snatched an automatic from his bathrobe pocket. Ever since he had become conscious of his surroundings he had insisted that it and his Spider kit, the small pack of tools he wore habitually strapped beneath his left arm, remain always with him as an additional protection against his enemies. He was desperately glad of it now. With a tap, he smashed the pane of glass. Resting the barrel on the sill, he rained lead down upon the men who raced toward the prostrate Easterner.

Two of the mob fell beneath his fusillade. A third staggered, reeled back to the protection of the crowd. Then Wentworth's gun was empty. He reloaded swiftly. The howling of the mob rose to a new pitch. The door slammed open behind him and his four police guards raced into the room.

"What is it, Mr. Wentworth? What is it?"

"They're killing a man in the streets," Wentworth snapped. "He's an Easterner. Save him!"

One of the cops cursed. "Serves him right," he growled. "Ought to kill 'em all."

But two of the men whirled and ran for the hall, while the other two fired down over the heads of the crowd. They wheeled Wentworth back from the window where he could see nothing but their broad blue backs, but he heard the cries that still rose from the mob.

"It's the yellow men!" came the shout. "The yellow men! They've got spies in the hospital!"

A few men yelled to storm the hospital but gradually the tenor of the cries changed.

"The consulate! The consulate! On to the consulate!" they chanted.

Wentworth stared straight ahead of him, wide-eyed, his gun still clenched in his hand. Here was cause for war. If the Eastern nation were so inclined, it might easily make capital of the attack on one of its nationals. If the consulate were stormed, nothing could prevent a declaration of hostilities. Justly, the East would demand reparation. Washington, harassed by the destruction of warships, by the piratical preying on its commercial fleet, would undoubtedly reply sharply. That mob must be turned from the consulate. The police....

"Nerts," said one of the cops at the window. "We ought to of let 'em string him up. Damn them! Sinking our ships, murdering our women and children...."

Crazy laughter bubbled up into Wentworth's throat, but he choked it down. Even the police were infected by the virus. The mad hysteria of war days had been revived. Only whisper that a man was of the alien race and immediately he was proscribed. No, he could expect small cooperation from the police. Even though their strength was thrown across the path of the march, officers, more in sympathy with the mob than against it, would be of little avail.

What was he waiting for? This was the task of the Spider, wasn't it? What did it matter that he was scarcely able to take a few tottering steps? The call had come. He had no choice but to answer.

Swiftly Wentworth seized the wheels of his chair, spun himself about, shot the chair into the hall. His long bony hands might tremble with weakness, but his will was indomitable. He must stem this march!

Down the hall, clad only in his pajamas and bathrobe, with a blanket tucked about his knees, Wentworth propelled the chair. No one interfered. The fury of shooting and mob had drawn all the workers who were free to the windows. Others were frantically calming frightened patients. As he reached the elevator, the door abruptly slammed open. Wentworth grabbed the wheels, stopped his chair with a jerk.

The white-coated elevator operator lay prostrate on the floor. Three men came barging out. One carried a sawed-off shotgun, the other two gripped automatics. Instantly, Wentworth understood. This was the reason the mob had marched by the hospital. D'Enry was striking again to rid himself of Wentworth's accusations, to strike down his nemesis. He had sent the mob to pull the guard from the door of Wentworth's room, then sent these three to kill him.

The leading man held the shot-gun ready.

Wentworth was so close to the elevator door that the killer almost stumbled over the wheel-chair. For a startled instant, he stared at the gaunt face of the Spider, then with a frightened curse, he jabbed the muzzle of the shot-gun forward.

CHAPTER 10
TO THE CONSULATE!

IN THAT instant, while the muzzle of the shotgun yawned at his face, Wentworth glimpsed death—glimpsed the doom of his country. It threw frantic strength into his enfeebled muscles. He swung his left arm against the muzzle. His automatic, pressed against the gunman's side, coughed out two muffled explosions.

Wentworth's fist closed over the shotgun; he tugged as the dying man's failing hands relaxed from it. It was split-second work to reverse the shotgun, to yank at its double triggers. The kick of the double discharge slammed Wentworth back in his chair. The thunderous echoes bellowed and clapped down the halls. Women screamed and an alarm bell began to ring stridently. One of the police guards thrust his head out into the hall. Wentworth straightened weakly.

The shotgun had done its deadly work. The remaining two gunmen had taken the full blast in their faces. The elevator was a sickening mess. Resolutely, Wentworth tugged at the wheels of his chair, maneuvered it into the cage and wrenched the lever. The car drifted downward as quietly as eiderdown. The only sounds were the distant hum of electric motors and Wentworth's own gasping breath. The alarms above grew faint.

The Spider's automatic lay on his knees. He patted it absently with his thin white hand which he presently raised to wipe the perspiration from his forehead. That had been close. He dropped the elevator to the basement, rolled his chair slowly out. The tires made dark red tracks along the white tiling of the hall. A closet opened to his right, showing blue rows of nurses' capes on hooks. Light gleamed in Wentworth's eyes. He caught down one of the capes, trundled on rapidly.

At the end of the corridor were double doors that opened onto the receiving platform of the hospital. Two men, remote from the noise and turmoil above, were wheeling a basket. Wentworth coasted up silently behind them as they opened the doors, revealed an ambulance backed up to the platform.

"Just a minute, boys," Wentworth said.

The men wheeled, stared into the muzzle of the automatic. Eyes flared wide in amazement.

"Never mind the corpse," said Wentworth. "I need the ambulance more."

At gun point, he shepherded the two men into the ambulance. Two other men were on the front seat, one in a driver's cap, the other a sedate undertaker with a black fedora funereally upon his head. Wentworth laughed out loud. He made the two hospital men close the doors, leveled his automatic at the two on the front seat.

"Get going fast!" he ordered. "Yank that siren on and keep it on."

The driver stared backward for one frightened instant, then gunned the ambulance into the drive, screaming on hot tires around a curve. The siren began to purr, moaned louder until it burst into a mad shriek. It swelled through the streets, slammed traffic to the curbs, opening a path for the mad dash of the ambulance.

Five blocks farther on, Wentworth stopped the ambulance long enough to force the two hospital attendants and the undertaker from it. He kept the man's black hat, started the driver going again. This time he told the man his destination. He echoed the cry of the mobs: "To the consulate!"

Wentworth laid the automatic on his knees and while the ambulance careened through the streets, he dug into the kit beneath his arm and dragged out the rudimentary make-up materials which he always carried. Rapidly he went to work on his face. He needed no mirror for this disguise. On his head he set a lank-haired black wig. His hands built a beak of a nose, stripped on shaggy brows, sallowed his skin. There was no need

109

to make his cheeks gaunt, to shadow the hollows beneath his eyes. His wound and his long illness had seen to that.

Not until his disguise was complete—until the nurse's cape was drawn about his shoulders and until the black hat was settled low over his eyes—did Wentworth look about him. Only two blocks to go now to the consulate. Dusk filled the canyons of the streets, early even for late fall. The sky was overcast and sullen with the leaden weight of unshed rains. It was half an hour before the street lights would go on. The ambulance spilled lights like blood from its red-sheathed head lamps.

WENTWORTH HAD no definite plan. His first frantic task had been to reach the consulate ahead of the mob. How he would cope with the pack when it bayed before the building he did not know. The ambulance squealed to a halt before an old-fashioned home that had been converted into offices for the Eastern power. It was red brick with a narrow porch and white graceful columns. Wide stone steps led up to the platform.

"Come back here," Wentworth ordered the driver.

The man came toward him slowly, eyes darting to his face, then away like frightened birds. Through the glass sides, Wentworth saw that one of two armed men in khaki who stood guard before the consulate was hurrying down the stone steps. He waited until the man appeared at the back of the ambulance.

"You two carry me up the steps to the doorway," he ordered. He presented his automatic so that both men might see.

The armed guard retreated a half step, hand dropping toward a holstered automatic at his thigh, but he reconsidered when the black eye of Wentworth's weapon focused on his forehead.

"Hurry," said Wentworth, "I have no time to waste. I bring a warning to the consul."

As driver and soldier caught hold of his chair, Wentworth began to talk swiftly. He must prevent them from thinking to drop the chair and so make him prisoner.

"A mob is coming to storm the consulate," he spoke swiftly. "As soon as you have taken me to the head of the steps, you, driver, call the police. Guard, you must warn the consul. I am going to do my best to stave off the attack, but there is no way of telling whether I will succeed."

While he spoke, the chair had been carried up the steps and placed on the small porch at its head. Wentworth settled himself against the cushions, hand still on his automatic.

"Hurry, driver," he ordered.

The ambulance man puzzled but obedient, ran down the steps, leaped to the door of his car. Wentworth turned to the soldiers. "Warn the consul," he urged, "then stay indoors. I can do much better with the mob if you do not show yourself."

"Say listen," snarled the soldier who had waited at the head of the steps. "Who the hell do you think you are, giving orders like that?"

Wentworth smiled slightly. These men were Americans, placed on guard here by the United States as a gesture of friendliness to the Eastern nation. They would know....

Light splashed up from Wentworth's hand from a small pocket flashlight and illuminated his face. The shadows made it weird, smeared darkness in the pits of his eyes where the pupils glowed like coals, emphasized the beaked nose, the shaggy brows beneath the down-drawn black hat. As the soldiers watched, the man in the chair seemed to become deformed. His shoulders became distorted, hunched up behind him so that his head jutted forward threateningly. Mocking, flat laughter rippled from Wentworth's lips.

"Shall I tell you who I am?" he asked jeeringly.

Abruptly, he thrust forward his right hand. On one finger, against a background of ebony black, a spot of red stood out like a living thing. It had sprawling hairy legs and venomous fangs. It was the ring of the Spider!

The soldier who had challenged Wentworth reeled back, with his arms thrown up defensively before him. The other cringed against the jamb of the door.

"Good God!" gasped the first soldier, "It's the Spider!"

Once more Wentworth's mocking laughter slid from his thin lips. He nodded twice, slowly. "Yes, the Spider," he mocked them. "Shall I repeat my orders, or…."

The men scrambled for the doorway, jerked it open and plunged inside. Wentworth was left alone on a small, high porch of the consulate. Through the twilight streets came the echoing roar of the mob. Within a few moments, police radio-cars would be thrown into their path. But this was no ordinary crowd to flee at the sight of a few bluecoats. As Wentworth had reason to know, it was led by the henchmen of D'Enry, of Miguel Oriano of the whip. It would take scores, hundreds of police or flashing points of bayonets to turn their march.

YET, ALONE, a dark huddled blotch against the white door, and columns of the consulate, Wentworth waited, a man almost helpless with the enfeeblement of long suffering, able to take only a few tottering steps without the aid of the wheelchair in which he sat. It had been a long time since he had assumed the garments and identity of Tito Caliepi, whom all the world knew as the Spider.

It was a desperate risk. Helpless to flee, the police closing about the spot where he sat, with his identity revealed to the armed men at his back, he had assumed this character. For by this means alone, he knew, did he stand any chance of turning the tide of attack that well might mean war for his country—war that the pirates plotted for their own secret and nefarious ends.

While he sat there, listening to the nearing approach of the mob howl, waiting for the first mad van to thrust into this peaceful street of old homes, Wentworth's mind raced back to the words he had overheard D'Enry utter in the river cabin. He frowned briefly. In some way, this plan for war would make the criminals rich. He thought again of that instant when D'Enry had confronted him with a drawn gun in the doorway of the cabin. How in God's name had the man divested himself of his bonds so quickly?

There was no time to ponder that now. He must prepare for the mob. A red glare showed at the corner a half block away, reflected on the white walls of an old church across the street—a glare from a torch carried at the head of the procession. Shouts and mad cries filled the street, drowning out the shrilling of police sirens as radio-cars rushed to intercept them.

Along the darkening street flowed the overwhelming tide of death. Wentworth could make out no features of the mob except the points of red fire where the torches flared. It was a sluggish monster with a thousand teeth, a hundred weapons of attack. Yet even such a monster must have a head… A thin smile distorted the Spider's face. The germ of an idea was growing in his fertile brain. His hands moved swiftly. He wrenched a pillow from behind him, thrust the muzzle of his automatic deep into it, then he touched the base of his cigarette lighter to the lens of his flashlight and printed there the red seal of the Spider.

The red torches were sputtering out one by one, the gray clouds seemed to rest upon the house tops, crowding darkness upon the city, packing it down into the streets. The few yellow lights that gleamed in windows along the walled way before the consulate only emphasized the desolation of blank-staring glass. A barren tree threshed in a rising wind, rasping skeleton arms together.

The mob writhed swiftly into the street, and reaching its goal, hesitated. Men's sharp exhorting voices rang out. It would not hesitate long. Within seconds, that great monster would swarm up these steps, would smash doors and burn, would murder and loot. If anyone noticed that black huddled figure in a wheel-chair on the porch, it did not seem to deter them.

Wentworth twisted up the lens of his flashlight, clicked the button, bathed his face in the edge of the dazzling white beam of light. It showed his gaunt features in sharp, shadowed relief. A sudden wave of silence struck the crowd. It spread slowly and Wentworth, sitting silent with his face bathed in light, waited motionless.

He had determined on his course now. His light with its

Spider seal, his muffled gun must do the work. If he failed, the Spider died, and with him died the peace hopes of a nation—perhaps the nation itself. As the silence widened its ripples over the mob, a few sharp voices spat curses at the ranks.

"It's only an old man," Wentworth heard one cry. "Are you afraid of an old man? These people have spat upon your country! They have killed your brothers, your wives, your children. They are fiends, beasts!"

The light left Wentworth's face, stabbed out into the crowd. It struck the white wall of the old church across the street and a gasp rose from the thick-pressed masses. Upon that vividly-white stone, the torch painted a circle of light, but its center was a thick black shadow, a shadow that had sprawling hairy legs and poised fangs, the shadow of a gigantic Spider!

THE LEADER'S sharp voice rose again; the light dropped from the wall, quested in the crowd. It found a man who stood head and shoulders above the serried ranks, a man poised upon a box who shouted of death and destruction to the enemy. As the light fell on him a shriek of wild laughter rang in the street, wild mocking laughter that was flat and ominous. The man who preached death staggered, threw his hands high. His shriek blended with the laughter, but it was the shriek of a man who was already dead.

The leader's body plunged down into the thick of the crowd, disappearing into the press, and the Spider shadow flitted back to the wall of the church. No man had heard a shot—the close-pressed pillow against the automatic's muzzle had hidden the flash and muffled the sound; Wentworth's shriek of laughter had drowned out what was left of the explosion—yet a man had died, died apparently because that weird Spider had brushed him!

"Death!" cried the Spider. "Death to those who preach death! That man died because he lied. He does not know the enemies of this country. No man knows—but the Spider knows! The Spider will avenge!"

The gusting breath of the mob picked up one word of what he said.

"Spider!" breathed a score of panicked men. The sound was a moan of fear, wonder, and awe.

After it came the sharp single cry of a man. "Kill him!" the man shrieked. "Kill the Spider! He's on the side of our enemies! On the side of the murderers! The Pirates!"

Once more the shadow of the Spider searched over the mob. Men flinched from the light as from a hail of death. Then once more the wild laughter of the Spider shrieked out over the mob, and a man died on his feet. There was a touch of hysteria in Wentworth's voice. He felt light-headed with his weakness.

"Death!" cried Wentworth. "Death to those that preach Death! Death to those that preach lies!"

Far up the street, he saw the headlights of a car swing wildly around a corner, heard the squeal of its brakes and heard the hoarse bellow of police. It made no impression on the thick of the mob bunched before Wentworth, held in the spell of the shadow that killed.

"It's just a man," a hoarse voice shouted in the midst of the mob. "He's shooting down our leaders! Kill him!"

A pistol cracked out in the darkness and lead whined past Wentworth, smacked into the door of the consulate.

A hysterical cry welled up from the mob. "Fool! Now the Spider will kill us all!" a woman screamed.

Wentworth swept his light to the spot whence a man had fired at him, saw that five men were beating another to death. The Spider's light lingered there until the five straightened, stood staring down at their ugly handiwork. Then once more it drifted slowly to the wall of the church where it rested.

"Go home!" cried the Spider. "Go home and think no more to take the law into your hands. I, the Spider, tell you that your dead shall be avenged. The Spider swears it!"

The oath of the Spider! Never had it been given and not fulfilled. The people knew it. If the Spider swore to kill a certain man in a certain way at a given time and place, he did it. What the Spider promised, he fulfilled. These people knew that.

"Go home!" the Spider boomed again. "I have sworn vengeance for you!"

A restless movement made itself felt in the ranks. In the distance, more police sirens shrieked. The mad hysteria of the crowd had been broken. No more were they drunk with the power of numbers. They began to think of individual safety, of police-courts and prisons and hard-swung night sticks. As abruptly as exploded powder, the mob began to scatter. Men and boys raced for dark alleys, women pulled their skirts high and made their high-heeled shoes beat the tattoo of retreat.

The Spider's work was done for the moment. It was time to go, to flee before the enclosing net of the police found him here.

Feebly, Wentworth eased from his wheel chair. He could not flee without it, could not get down the stairs. He leaned a hand against a pillar and sent the chair bounding down the steps. He went heavy-footed after it.

Behind him a door slammed open and the two soldiers rushed out with their automatics in their hands. Around a corner three blocks away whirled the headlights of another car. Its siren announced it as a police-roadster. Suddenly, the long-delayed street lights blazed on. Death on all sides for the Spider, death for the man who had just saved the lives of the consul and his staff, had thwarted a fiendish plot.

CHAPTER 11
RAM SINGH CALLS

AS THE two soldiers rushed close, Wentworth spattered the rays of his Spider shadow light in their faces. They threw up their hands. "Keep that damned voodoo light off of me," one howled. "I'm just trying to help you!"

Wentworth frowned, contorting his brow heavily. Was this a trick to catch him? His brain was reeling with weakness. He could not think… He switched off his light.

"Very well," his voice rasped. "Take me to my wheel chair. But remember, at the first sign of treachery, the light…."

"Okay, okay," the soldier agreed. "Quick, now, before the cops get here."

The two soldiers took Wentworth gingerly by the arms, helped his awkward stumbling feet to the chair. The Spider

118

sank into it gratefully, eased his aching back into its cushions. The wound in his chest was throbbing like the slow push of a hot knife into his flesh. "Thanks," he said dully. "I won't forget this."

"Sure you will, buddy," growled the soldier. "Don't you think I know that if you hadn't turned that mob, I'd have had to take the rap out front myself?"

He reached out a hand as if to clap Wentworth on the shoulder, hesitated, then gave the chair a gentle push instead.

"Good luck, Spider," the soldier called softly.

Wentworth's thin hands dropped over the arms of the chair. Behind him he heard brakes squeal as the police car halted.

Wentworth turned a corner slowly, wheeled off into the shadows. He was smiling despite the pain and weakness, despite the uncertainty of what the next minute held and the deep mystery of the criminals behind all this murder and suffering. Not everyone, it seemed, was ungrateful to the Spider....

It was three quarters of an hour later that a taxi drew to a halt before the Fifth Avenue apartment in which Wentworth had his penthouse. The driver alighted hurriedly, summoned help. The doorman and two hall boys came to his call. They helped a thin, feeble man across the sidewalk, into his private elevator, supported him until he sank upon a luxurious davenport in his own living room.

Old Jenkyns shooed them out hurriedly, distributing money among them liberally. Then he came back to Wentworth quickly, his wrinkled old face showing a bewildering mixture of happiness over his return and anxiety over his condition. Wentworth smiled at him, his head lolling back upon the cushions.

"Call Miss Nita, Jenkyns," Wentworth instructed. "Then mix me one of your famous specials. When I've got that under my belt…" His voice trailed off.

His doctor, a while later, muttered in his beard, but could find no serious ill effects of Wentworth's having left the hospital under his own power. Wentworth laughed at his dire warnings, smiled across at Nita's worried eyes. When the doctor had gone, Wentworth became completely serious. At his stern insistence, he was brought newspapers of the entire period of his sickness. He skimmed hurriedly through the records of the country's growing madness.

"But, Dick," Nita protested, "you can't possibly do anything in your present condition. This is ridiculous. You must get your strength back…" Wentworth smiled at her quizzically, sent Jenkyns for the latest paper. When it had come, he tossed it into her lap. The headline read:

SPIDER SAVES CONSUL FROM THREATENING MOB

"You see, dear," said Wentworth softly. "Even an old feeble Spider can sting. Death can wait, but my service to my country and my people cannot."

THE BELL at the door buzzed faintly and Wentworth stiffened, remembering suddenly what had occurred the last time the faithful Jenkyns had answered such a summons, the invasion of armed gangsters that had followed. He snaked out his gun, held it ready. Jenkyns entered, a letter on a silver tray.

"Special delivery, sir," he said.

Wentworth frowned at the tray, then abruptly he snatched the letter and tore it open with hands that trembled.

"Ram Singh!" he cried.

The letter contained a single line of Hindustani characters: *"Come to the island."*

"Good old Ram Singh," he said. "He has stuck to the trail. I don't know why he hasn't communicated before, but this makes up for everything. To the island it is!"

"But, Dick…."

Wentworth smothered Nita's protest with an arm about her shoulders and a kiss upon her lips. Within three hours, Jackson had fueled a large cabin plane and Wentworth was speeding southward. Their first stop would be Miami, Florida.

Wentworth was not going to rescue Ram Singh, but to strike a blow directly at the headquarters of the pirate crew who for their own evil ends were seeking to wreak disaster upon the United States.

Before he left the country, Wentworth had sent to all the newspapers a statement signed by the seal of the Spider in which he outlined all that he knew about the pirates and blamed them for the attempt to throw the country into war.

The thing he had blocked—the sacking of the consulate—was but an echo of the violence that everywhere racked the country. Especially upon the West Coast had the people run amuck. Military law had been declared in California and guards patrolled the streets with fixed bayonets to prevent an irrevocable act on the part of the citizens against the nationals of the East.

Truly no time could be lost in striking at the pirate leaders if Wentworth were to save the country. Yet, he could make no plans. He could only rest, build his strength during the thirty-six hours before they could reach the island.

Jackson, using a robot pilot, handled the ship alone, snatching occasional cat-naps while Wentworth kept an eye on the instrument panel. The plane was twelve hours south of Miami, two thirds of the way to the island, when the radio brought Wentworth the information that the President had summoned the Congress into special session "to consider the present international crisis."

Wentworth, hands clenched as he listened to the staccato announcement over the air, realized that the country was on the point of declaring war. But that war must not be declared, and Wentworth knew that only he could avert it.

"There must be no war," he muttered grimly. Especially there must be no war for the selfish purposes of this pack of murderers who conspired to cause it. The special session of Congress was called for two days hence. He had forty-eight—sixty hours to smash this piratical gang. Sixty hours to destroy single-handed a conspiracy that was strong enough to draw the United States to the brink of war! And twelve of those hours would be lost merely in flying to the spot where he was to launch the battle.

HE GLANCED out the window at the flashing diamond brilliance of the waters below, the blue Caribbean reflecting the noonday sun. At least it would be dark when they neared the island. Wentworth planned to drop to the water safely out of hearing of the pirates there, and taxi to land. The sound of the plane's powerful engines would be much less easily detected from the surface than from high in the air.

By this means, he hoped to surprise the pirates and slip ashore unobserved. Once there, he would make plans. Thank heavens, his strength was returning rapidly. Thoughtfully he touched his pocket, fingered a small packet of stimulants. When his strength gave out, they would keep him going for a while….

The night was moonless but clear when they slanted down toward the surface of the sea. They dared not use a magnesium flare, but faintly the waters were visible as they mirrored the stars and flashed now and then with the green spatter of phosphorescence as some fish leaped. Jackson dropped the plane inches at a time, feeling for the water and finally, with masterly skill, touched his skids and cut the motor. The great ship settled as gracefully as a bird. Minutes later, motors turning slowly, they began to creep toward the island.

It was slow work and only after two hours did the dark loom of land ahead tell them their journey was near an end. The motors were cut entirely now and Jackson prepared to launch a rubber raft for the final lap to the beach.

Abruptly, from the blackness of the night, blue-white searchlights poured their dazzling glare! With a heart shudder of apprehension, Wentworth saw that the lights were focused from three sides and bathed the plane from stem to stern.

"Welcome, Spider!" a man boomed through a megaphone. "Congratulations, *Señor*, on the speed of your trip. Do not attempt to escape. There are three batteries of six-pounders trained on you at point-blank range!"

123

The boat from which the man spoke drew nearer and Wentworth detected the purr of electric engines. He had made this flight only to fall at the beginning of the venture into the hands of the criminals. What hope would he have now, weakened as he was, of escaping? And twelve—no, fourteen!—of the sixty hours that remained to him had already elapsed.

Woodenly he listened to the pirate's orders. He and Jackson got in the small rubber boat and Jackson began to paddle them toward the speaker. How had the pirates known of his arrival? How had they been able to trap him so perfectly? He guessed the answer, though, and a moment later, the deep voice of the man on the boat confirmed it.

"Miguel Oriano speaking, *Señor* Spider," he called. "What do you think of the little trick of having Ram Singh write a letter? Clever, eh what? We could have killed you in New York, *Señor* Spider, but it seemed to me better that you come to the island where we have crude, but effective, entertainment."

Grimly, Wentworth forced his lips to smile into the glare of the blue-white light.

"I still live," he told himself, "and while I live…."

Miguel Oriano seemed to read his thoughts: "I shall have to let you live for a while, *Señor* Spider, to regain your strength. I would not want to cheat you of any enjoyment—when I wield the whip!"

CHAPTER 12
IN THE PIRATE PRISON

THE THREAT of Miguel Oriano boomed flatly across the waters. The silence that followed was as ominous as death. Jackson paddled their awkward, round-ended craft slowly on into the eye of the searchlight. Wentworth, facing him, saw that his wide jaws were set stubbornly.

"I've got my gun between my knees," said Jackson softly, speaking without moving his lips. "How's for shooting out that light...."

Wentworth smiled faintly. A hundred methods of escape had already raced through his brain but aside from his physical weakness, there remained one cogent argument against the attempt. He knew nothing of the situation on the island, was unacquainted with its topography. As a fugitive, he would be heavily handicapped, both in spying out the land and in working out an attack, for the whole island would be on his heels.

"No, Jackson," he said. "We should stand small chance of getting away from all three boats. It is better to wait. And don't forget we have an ally ashore. Ram Singh is here."

Jackson's mouth shut more grimly. In silence, he paddled the rubber boat gently against the ladder lowered over the side of the electric-launch. Rough hands seized them, stripped them of weapons, found, too, Wentworth's secret tool-kit and removed it.

Miguel Oriano, the leather plait of his whip coiled about his forearm, strode through the circle of men who held Wentworth and Jackson. He was resplendently garbed in black velvet, bell

125

trousers slashed with silver, a silver-ornamented jacket to match. The peaked Mexican sombrero on his head shone with metal.

"Ah, *Señor* Spider," he swept an elaborate bow, "welcome to our island."

Wentworth shrugged at the mockery, glanced about him casually. Fully a dozen men ringed him and Jackson, revolvers ready. It was fortunate indeed, Wentworth thought, that Ram Singh was on hand to help, otherwise their chances of escape would be remote.

The electric-launch was already purring forward, he discovered, slitting the phosphorescent waters toward a flashing red beacon. The searchlight of Oriano's craft swung to the shore and illuminated an elaborate concrete pier and warehouses. Beyond the docks, houses shone whitely; windows were yellow squares.

"We are quite comfortably situated here," Oriano assured him, suave at his elbow. "Our guest house is nice, too. The bars are manganese steel, the locks the best obtainable." He broke off in his deep, gusty laughter.

Wentworth smiled politely, but his heart was a weight in his chest. Even with Ram Singh's help, he might have difficulty in freeing himself from his prison before Congress met and took the irrevocable step of declaring war. One thing seemed clear. If the island was used this openly as a headquarters for the pirates, there no longer was any doubt of Don Estéban's guilt. His must be the brain behind all these operations.

THE LAUNCH edged to the dock and floodlights blazed out. Wentworth was marched ashore with a guard of six men about him, all carrying drawn pistols and the native heavy-bladed *machetes*.

Jackson was similarly watched. As they advanced, another party came to meet them. At the head walked a figure at sight of whom Wentworth's heart gave a great bound. It was Ram Singh, resplendent in the white he loved, a spotless turban upon his dark, arrogant head.

Behind Ram Singh, Mexicans padded respectfully. It was obvious that he was no prisoner, but a man of rank. Ram Singh's swarthy face broke into a sneering smile. He strode straight up to Wentworth—spat upon him!

"Dog!" snarled Ram Singh. "Soon you shall pay in full!"

Miguel Oriano bellowed again with laughter, smiting Wentworth painfully between the shoulders.

"A pleasant surprise for you, *Señor*. We have convinced Ram Singh that he will best serve himself by serving us. That was how it was so easy to trap you."

Wentworth's mind reeled beneath the impact of this last blow. If Ram Singh had turned against him, what was left? He heard numbly the savage curses that Jackson poured out upon the Hindu. He scarcely realized when the door of his cell clanged metallically upon him. He sank woodenly upon the hard bench that was his sole furniture.

Finally his tormentors left and Jackson, from the adjoining cell, attempted to encourage him.

"Don't mind the heathen going back on you, Major," he urged. "He was bound to do that some day. We'll crack this can wide open and take these boys."

Ram Singh could not be counted on. He remembered that before Ram Singh was hypnotized into an attack on him. Wentworth drove bitterness from his mind. He must think only of escape.

Slowly Wentworth revolved plans, but an hour later he was no nearer solution than at the start.

Abruptly, the prison burst into a bedlam of confused shouting. Wentworth dragged himself to the door hopefully. From the third tier, where his cell was located, he peered down into the well between the blocks of steel cages. He could make out only that front door of the prison had opened and that a considerable company of persons had entered. He strained his ears to distinguish the cause of the shouting. He caught pleas of mercy. He heard a woman calling down blessings upon the head of— *Señorita* Carmencita!

Wentworth watched and listened, saw that the procession was ascending. It passed the second tier. Could she be coming to his cell? He fought down the drumming of his pulses. Even if she did, it brought no hope. The noisy confusion continued.

The procession reached the third tier and now he could see the lovely girl he had last met amid the gayety of the *St. Delroy* Roof. She was pacing sedately down the steel passageway directly toward him. She came on and stopped opposite his cell, turned slowly to face him.

WENTWORTH SAW with a sense of shock that she was dressed completely in black. A lacy mantilla was draped from a high comb upon her jet-black locks and fell gracefully over her shoulders, strengthening the pallor of her oval face. There was grief in her dark eyes.

"Open the door," she said slowly, "so that I may confront the murderer of my brother."

The words struck Wentworth with stunning force. Then D'Enry had succeeded finally in his efforts to murder André, the son of the Don! More than that, he had contrived to fasten the guilt for his crime upon the Spider!

Wentworth stepped back a pace and the grating swung outward. Grouped behind Carmencita were a half dozen heavily-armed peons. They glared at him, holding the weapons ready. There was no chance to escape.

Wentworth's eyes rose to the girl's face. She seemed even lovelier than before in the habiliments of her mourning. Her hands were as white as magnolia blossoms. For long minutes, she stood gazing at Wentworth without speaking. He saw that, strangely, her eyes were not accusing, that their liquid depths seemed to flash some message to him.

"Why did you do it?" she asked finally, her voice deep as a bell note. "Why did you kill André? He was a hot-headed boy, but not dangerous." As she spoke, Wentworth saw that a small package wrapped in black was being lowered slowly from her hands by a thread, dropping gradually toward the floor. He jerked his eyes quickly from it to her face, saw that she nodded slightly. What was this? He kept his face expressionless.

"I cannot understand," Carmencita went on, "why a man would do such a thing. Can't you tell me?"

Wentworth bowed low. *"Señorita,"* he said, "I know of no

reason why any man should kill André. I did not do it. I have only hatred and contempt for the man who did."

"You say you did not do it?" the girl's voice was sorrowful. The package had reached the floor at her feet. She dropped the thread by which it had been lowered, bowed her head. "If you take that attitude, there is nothing I can say. I had hoped you would be repentant…."

She turned abruptly, the close ranks of her guards opened for her and the door clanged heavily shut. Wentworth crowded against the grating and watched her. Why was the girl so friendly that apparently she was willing to frustrate her father's plans for his execution? Obviously she had intended her words to convey to him both the information that André was dead and that he was to be accused of the crime. But the package….

Wentworth forced himself to stand motionless watching while the girl and her guards descended to the main floor and filed out through the great main doors of the prison. Then he snatched up the small black package. He could not prevent a slight trembling of his hands as he untied it. Jackson was pressed against the bars, staring.

The package resisted Wentworth's fumbling fingers, then abruptly it opened, revealed a small bottle wrapped in a piece of white paper. There was no light in his cell. He held the paper to the rays slating through the bars.

"When you are free," read the note, written in a rounded, childish writing, "come to me at the main house. Ram Singh will be waiting outside. The bottle contains acid. He said you would know how to use it."

Twice Wentworth skimmed through the note before the words registered in his brain, then he barely suppressed a cry of triumph. Ram Singh was faithful! Why had he ever doubted the loyal Hindu? Naturally, Ram Singh had been forced to pretend hatred and scorn.

It came to him only after moments of jubilation that this acid must be some of that perfected by the chemical wizard who assisted him, Professor Brownlee, which would eat through steel as rapidly and readily as a hot knife through butter. Wentworth's own supply had been taken from him in the kit when he had been captured. With this acid, it would be the work of minutes only to break the lock and escape. And Ram Singh and the daughter of the Don would fight with him!

Swiftly, Wentworth told Jackson what had happened. Jackson cursed once softly and with feeling, then was silent. Wentworth crossed to the door and skillfully feeding the acid into the lock, soon was able to force open his cell. He repeated the trick on Jackson's door, then they slipped down the steel corridor toward the stairs. They were still unarmed and guards kept watch below, but the Spider felt the buoyancy of success in his veins. Nothing could stop him now! With Ram Singh and Carmencita to help, he might soon be able to smash the power of the pirates here, race back to Washington….

CHAPTER 13
FORWARD—OR DIE!

A T THE foot of the stairs, Jackson slugged a guard and snatched keys from his belt. Wentworth snapped out lights while Jackson manipulated the locks of the main door.

"Let's go," he said.

The door opened a crack and he slipped out.

The moon had pushed a tardy white face above the dark hills that flanked the town. Coral walls glistened in ghostly luminance. The dark tall palms shadowed the door, but across the square torches did an exciting fire-fly dance.

Just above his breath, Wentworth whistled a weird five-noted tune. Its echo came faintly from the night where shrubbery clustered close to the prison wall. In the shadows the white loom of a crouching man guided them.

The silent man in white flitted ahead, let them deftly through thickets past a line of white glistening huts. As the ground began to rise beneath their feet, there was a sudden uproar behind. Their escape had been discovered. Another two hundred yards and they slipped through a narrow, iron gate into a garden walled with coral, then into a great, high ceilinged hall. It was dimly lighted by spaced candles, and here the man in white confronted them for the first time. It was Ram Singh.

Without a word he flung himself to his knees, touched his forehead to the floor before Wentworth in extreme obeisance—his apology for even appearing to have turned against his master.

"It is well, Ram Singh," Wentworth said softly. "I understand. There is nothing but honor in what you have done."

Behind, the noisy alarms grew louder. Jackson stepped forward silently and offered his hand. Ram Singh clasped it and his white teeth flashed in a smile. These two were warriors who respected each other.

With a salaam then, Ram Singh led on. They crossed a patio. Wentworth saw that they were going to the private quarters of Carmencita!

At a portal of slatted blinds, Ram Singh knocked out a rhythmic signal. Instantly the door opened and they were ushered into the presence of the *señorita*.

There was something regal about her as she received them. She sat with folded hands in the middle of a large room. The gleaming dark floor was bare; the walls were hung in rich tapestries. The lights were soft, but their shadowing, more than the brilliant glare of the prison, revealed how grief had worn the girl's face. In a corner, a candle flickered before a niched statue of the Virgin.

"I am here to assist you," Wentworth said. "Where is your father?"

HER STORY came men in a swift rush. André had never returned from the duel. Haillie had put him ashore, found a cab for him at his request. Hours later, her brother's body had been found on the banks of the river. Her father suspected D'Enry. He had brought Carmencita and her mother to the island, then gone back to America for vengeance.

"But there are mysterious things going on here," said

He lifted his sword and pointed it at Oriano. "There is my betrayer!" he thundered. "Kill the dog!"

Carmencita rapidly, "things I do not understand. It was my father's wish that Miguel Oriano remain in charge, but I am afraid of that man. If it were not for my faithful *muchachos…*" she broke off, controlled her obvious agitation. "When Ram Singh told me of you, I decided to ask you to come. Ram Singh maneuvered it through Oriano. We thought it would be impossible for you to land without being detected—thought it better that you be taken prisoner at once."

Wentworth nodded. The strategy was sound, typical of the Hindu.

"Miguel Oriano rules by fear and his whip," the girl was still speaking. "I do not think my father knows that. He would not approve. He is a stern man, but just and kind to the peons. They would gladly die for him."

An abrupt smile twitched at Wentworth's lips. He knew now how he could smash this pirate nest.

"*Señorita,*" he broke in on her speech. "Will you get for me the finest suit your father has on the place? The more Mexican, the more spangled with silver, the better. Get me also a picture of him. Ram Singh, do you still have your kit? Good. Now, tell me briefly how Don Estéban speaks to his peons, how he summons them to him…."

A half hour later, traveling by the same route by which they had approached the house, they dodged a search party going toward the Don's mansion. They stole to the harbor, seized and bound three guards and paddled silently out to a huge plane moored a short distance from the shore. It took a full hour to tow it down the coast out of sight of the town. Once there, Jackson whined the motors into life, sent the ship northward, low over the waters, all lights extinguished.

Twenty minutes later, a plane with all lights blazing circled over the harbor and flashed a signal. Flood-lights illumined the water before the docks and the plane slanted to a landing beside a huge hangar. A tall bearded man alighted on the ramp. He was clad in black velvet and where the garments of Miguel Oriano had been slashed and ornamented with silver, his were garnished with gold and jewels. A golden sword swung at his side. The peons on the docks swept off their hats.

"*Viva!*" they cried, waving their sombreros. "*Viva Don Estéban!*"

Wentworth, for it was he in disguise as Don Estéban, permitted his bearded lips to relax in a grave smile, then he called an imperative order that the great bell be rung.

Within moments after he had landed, the violent clangor of a great brazen bell swelled over the island. Men and women rushed to the great square before the prison where, bathed in white light, the resplendent figure of Don Estéban stood waiting. Miguel Oriano was among the first to arrive, striding through the few who had assembled, his whip swinging from his wrist. He stalked jauntily up to where Wentworth stood.

"What's all the big noise about?" he demanded insolently.

WENTWORTH MADE no verbal answer, but his sword leaped from its sheath, the flat of it smacked Miguel Oriano across the cheek. Oriano reeled back with an oath, his face hideous with rage.

From the shadows, Ram Singh darted in front of Went-

137

worth with a drawn revolver. Jackson raised a rifle. For seconds it seemed Oriano would hurl himself forward in spite of this defense. He snatched out a silver whistle, piped on it twice.

The square was crowded with people now and a wash of murmuring voices beat against the enclosing white buildings. Wentworth raised his hands for silence. In the light his naked sword flashed.

"My children," he cried in the deep, imperious voice of Don Estéban. "I have been betrayed!"

An utter hush fell upon the assembled people, a hush in which the soft rustle of the palms that stood before the prison became audible. Miguel Oriano stood stiffly, the whip dangling, staring with incredulous eyes at the figure upon the prison steps. As yet, no one had answered that whistle blast.

"In my absence," rang out the Den's sonorous voice again, "a dog I trusted has turned upon me and destroyed my flocks. He has used my substance for his own ends. He has blackened my name with crime."

Rising voices rippled across the square. Angry cries rose sharply. Men tossed their clenched fists into the air.

"Name the dog!" men cried. "Name this blackener of thy honored name!"

Wentworth stood silent, the sword still in his hand, but pointing now toward the ground at his feet. He turned slowly toward where Miguel Oriano stood. The whip-master was no longer alone. Men had slipped secretly through the shadows and flanked him, men with rifles and drawn revolvers, with bare *machetes* in their hands. They were few in number and their faces were villainous. With them stood a dozen white men and in their forefront was the pilot Norska whose trickery had nearly defeated the Spider in his first brush with the pirates.

As Wentworth faced this tight small group of men, Oriano stepped forward and cracked his whip with a crash like a revolver shot.

"Hear me!" he bellowed. "This man is not Don Estéban! He is the Spider who killed the young Don!"

He flung up his left hand and fired a revolver point blank at Wentworth. Wentworth wavered a little, but stood firm. His sword pointed at Oriano with a gleam like fire.

"There is my betrayer!" he thundered. "Miguel Oriano! Kill the dog!"

Before the last syllable had poured from his mouth, there was a concerted rush upon the knot of desperate men who had rallied behind Oriano.

Ram Singh leaped forward to the attack. His great, long-bladed knife flashed in the air, but Oriano dived suddenly to the protection of the bodies of his men. Jackson sprang to Wentworth's side.

"It's all right," Wentworth said quietly. "Luckily, he aimed for my body. Don Estéban's bullet-proof vest stood me in good stead."

He was staring out over the square where the blazing white lights fought back the darkness, where dark men in sombreros fought with other dark men. *Machetes* flashed in the brilliant glare and men screamed out their lives in pain. But the defiant knot of pirates did not stand long against the attack.

ORLANO'S FLIGHT before the threat of Ram Singh's knife had broken their morale and they soon joined him in flying to safety through the darkness. Within minutes, the square was deserted but for a scattered half-dozen bodies that sprawled with the inertness of rag dolls upon the stone pavement. Wentworth turned to Ram Singh.

"Summon the girl, Carmencita, from the house," he said. "Within a short time, we must fly to the United States. I think she will want to join her father there. Jackson, come with me."

He strode off, still in the imperious manner of Don Estéban toward the docks, listening to the distant crackle of gunfire as it dwindled toward the dark hills behind the town. The Don's peons, he knew, would wipe out those vermin to the last man. They would pay for their crimes as completely as if the Spider himself had executed the vengeance.

As he neared the hangars where the sea-planes rested, there came an abrupt burst of firing from within, followed instantly by the roar of heavy motors. Wentworth jerked out his automatic, hurried forward as fast as his limited strength would permit. Evidently some of the pirates had escaped the vengeful peons. Jackson raced on ahead, rifle at body. But while they were still a hundred yards distant, a plane slithered down the ramp to the water and struck in a shower of spray. Jackson dropped to one knee and pumped swift bullets at the ship, but it bellowed off toward the north, skimming faster and faster over the surface of the sea.

Jackson sprang on toward the hangar and when Wentworth came up, he was working furiously over another plane. He got the motor started, maneuvered the ship on its wheeled truck toward the broad doors.

"The damned scoundrels got away!" he roared above the reverberating engines. "Miguel Oriano and half a dozen others. The Mexican over there said before he died that they had all the money with them. Millions!"

Wentworth turned heavily, gazed back toward the brilliantly lighted square where men's bodies lay in the last surrender of death. Across it Ram Singh and Carmencita were hurrying.

"We'll lose them," Jackson cried urgently. "They'll get away!"

The fugitive plane still showed a speck of light on the horizon when the Hindu and the girl scrambled aboard the ship. Wentworth swung in behind them, nodded to Jackson and instantly the plane slid down the runway, took the water and roared off into the northern sky.

Wentworth's jaw locked grimly beneath the bearded disguise of Don Estéban. Even if they overtook and destroyed that fleeing plane, he would not have reached the end of the trail.

Wentworth strode to Jackson's side. "I want Miguel Oriano— *alive,*" he said. A grim smile crossed his bearded lips. "There are certain questions I want to ask him."

CHAPTER 14
THE WHIP OF ORIANO

A LONG chase is a stern chase, and the two planes were of equal power and both well piloted. In the end it was the lighter load of Wentworth's Sikorsky—when the sun had coursed across the sky and drawn near to the horizon again—that brought them on the tail of the pirate ship just as the dark smudge of the Florida mainland hove above the meeting line of sea and sky.

Neither ship was equipped with machine guns, but Wentworth took Jackson's rifle and going into the cockpit, poked a small hole through the forward glass. Instantly the huge transport ahead of them side-slipped frantically. It was obvious they were watching closely.

Jackson threw the wheel forward with the quickness of thought to follow. Bracing the rifle, Wentworth began a slow and careful fire, directed not at the cockpit or the cabin, but at the giant twin motors braced above the plane. He was firing a powerful weapon of high velocity, a steel-jacketed bullet. Jackson followed the pirate ship as if tied to its tail.

They were streaking along now at two thousand feet, within a half-mile of the Florida coast. Once more Wentworth took careful aim and fired. Abruptly the ship ahead staggered, ducked downward in a screaming dive. With a thin smile, Wentworth put down the rifle.

"Remember," he called above the thunder of the motors, "*I want Oriano alive!*"

The pirate ship slowly settled to the sea, skimmed with swiftly-dying momentum toward the shore. It ploughed to a stop a hundred yards from shore, and Jackson skillfully drew to a halt half way between it and the white, glistening beach.

"Surrender!" Wentworth shouted across the water. "Surrender, or we'll blow you out of the water."

A burst of gunfire answered him. Bullets ripped small bright holes through the metal sides of the ship. Carmencita uttered a single frightened cry, then lay flat on the floor at Wentworth's order. He brought out his rifle again. Once more he aimed not at the occupants of the ship, but at the Sikorsky's mechanism—at the gasoline tank! Deliberately he pumped the entire magazine of shells through the tank, then he shouted again:

"The next bullets I fire will be incendiary! You will be blown up! Do you surrender?"

He had no incendiary bullets, but the pirates had no way of telling that. The door of the other ship flung open suddenly. Men dived, one after another, into the blue depths. Wentworth watched keenly to spot Miguel Oriano, but the men were all garbed alike in khaki and he could not detect their identities.

"Beach the plane," he shouted to Jackson and the motors picked up their song again, shoved the plane high and dry upon the beach. Wentworth had counted seven men leaping from the plane. His own party was only three, but the advantage of position was all with him.

A HUNDRED feet out, the waters shallowed abruptly so swimmers would not have the protection of the sea from that point. Neither could they advance swiftly, but would be forced to flounder and splash to where guns menaced them from the waiting plane. But only four men came directly toward the shore. The others divided, two striking southward along the beach, one fighting stubbornly northward against the tide.

Jackson waited for the four who came together. Ram Singh raced south to meet the two who fled that way, and Wentworth, still in the garb of Don Estéban, strode his resplendent way to take the seventh man. There was a tight smile on his mouth that pulled the lips away from his teeth. Who but Miguel Oriano would swim thus stubbornly alone and against the tide?

For nearly two miles, the man Wentworth paced fought the currents before the black triangular fins of cruising sharks drove him to the shallows. He came inward slowly and Wentworth saw as the man rose that it was indeed Oriano. His craggy, ugly face was thrust forward, his whip coiled about his forearm.

Miguel Oriano came forward in a slow, almost solemn pace. As he came, he drew the pliant long plait of his whip through his hands. If he had carried a firearm, apparently he had cast it off during his swim. He was naked to the waist and his ragged trousers reached only to his knees. The bulge and ripple of his muscles showed and as he drew closer, the evil, sneering grin upon his pock-marked face. The ruff of his hair was smeared down upon his forehead.

Wentworth trod lightly across the ankle-deep softness of the dry sand to the firm stretch where the waves had washed. There he waited. His weapon was the jeweled sword of Don Estéban.

"Greetings," Oriano called from the surf as he floundered steadily nearer. "Greetings and congratulations, *Señor* Spider. You turned a neat trick on the island. That was fine shooting from the air, but you have overplayed your hand now. In fact, I think...."

As a comma for his sentence, his hand jerked suddenly upward and forward and the lash of the whip flicked forward, striking snake-like for Wentworth's face!

But Wentworth had been watching the coiled leather, watching the wrist that wielded it. He fell easily on guard with his sword tip outthrust. As the whip streaked forward, he cut with a swift, dragging motion of its sabre edge. With an oath, Oriano arrested the striking tip of his whip in mid-blow, snatched it clear of the threat of that keen edge. The sword would have sliced through it.

In the same motion, Oriano sent the lash writing forward again, this time with a different purpose. If those coils caught the blade or arm now, they would twine about it mercilessly and Wentworth would be without a weapon, helpless in the hands of a ruthless murderer. But the Spider had a defense for that, too. He sprang lightly backward. His right arm remained rigidly extended, but the sword was now drawn back to slash.

Once more Oriano flicked back his whip from danger, rage distorting his face. He caught the lash in his hands and held it coiled supple before him. During the brief flurry of attack and parry, he had waded from the water and stood now on parity with Wentworth upon the sands. Muscles were knotted across the man's chest; his breathing was even and regular. He had profited by that slow advance across the shallows.

Wentworth's own breath came in gulps, there was a singing of blood in his temples. He must conquer this cunning man—and quickly. Death was grinning at him with a pock-marked face, death for himself—and disaster for the country.

WITH A twist and a shoulder-wrench, Oriano struck again, but this time it was the slender lash-tip he held in his hand. The lead-loaded butt of his whip flew through the air straight at

Wentworth's head. No touch of the blade would turn this blow, no slash could sever it and avert the doom. There was too much strength behind the throw, too much weight in the club itself.

Wentworth dropped to his knee beneath the direct line of the cast. Instantly he knew the maneuver had been a mistake. Oriano had only to twitch the lash to bring the club crashing down up on his head. Desperately, Wentworth thrust upward with the point of his sabre. He made no attempt to slash with the sharp edge of the blade. Instead, he thrust at the leather thong at the handle's base.

His long years of practice on the dueling strips stood him in good stead. Truly, his blade slipped through the loop. At the same instant, Wentworth jerked backward, exerting strain in the same direction the club was flying. Oriano let out a surprised cry. The lash jerked from his hands, and following the swing of the handle, whirling on the axis of the blade, swished in a wide circle and fell behind Wentworth. Instantly, the Spider sprang to his feet again.

He dropped the sword and seized the handle. Oriano flung himself forward in a desperate charge and the whip, his own whip, whined through the air. The lash flicked across his chest. With a screech of rage, Oriano checked his mad charge, reeled backward. A red furrow welted across his chest where the lash had brushed.

For a moment, Oriano stood panting with rage, staring while Wentworth slowly coiled the whip before him. Miguel knew the virtues of his own weapon, feared it as can only a man who knows the thing he himself has created. Abruptly, the pirate pivoted, started to race away from the enfeebled Spider.

Once more the lash sang through the air and Oriano screamed as he felt it bite into his ankle. It twined about his leg, pitched him headlong into the sand. Wentworth twitched the whip free and Oriano sprang up again. He was blind with panic now. Once more he tried to run and once more Wentworth spilled him to earth as a man might break a horse with a lasso.

The pirate was past reason now. He flung to his feet, whirled and charged savagely at this mocking figure in velvet.

Once more, almost slowly, Wentworth whirled the whip about his head. He struck and the lash thwacked on Oriano's corded throat. Its small end wrapped entirely around and Wentworth threw the last ounce of his strength into a two-handed heave on the handle. The lash tightened its grip. Oriano seized the plait, his mouth gasping wide without sound. His eyes strained in their sockets. He pitched face down in the sand, writhing.

Wentworth waited calmly until Oriano's movements grew weak, until they ceased, then with a twitch of the handle, he yanked the lash from the throat of the man he had mastered. Throughout the fight he had heard shots and now, turning, he saw that Ram Singh was loping across the sands toward him. Wentworth nodded. This phase of the battle was won. Now, when Oriano talked....

Arms bound before him, he herded the revived Oriano back toward the plane. His companions lay dead upon the sands, all save one held at rifle point by Jackson. It was the pilot Norska.

147

The loot had been transferred to Wentworth's plane. At Wentworth's orders, Ram Singh tossed a line over a slanting palm. He noosed the end about Oriano's wrists, hauled the rope taut so that the pirate leader stood with arms strained upward, toes nearly clear of the ground.

"If I remember correctly, Miguel *mío,*" he said softly, "your description of this whip was 'crude but effective.' Do you want to talk now—or later?"

AS HE finished speaking, he rolled the whip off into distance, cracked it loudly. Oriano winced. His head sagged backward. "What do you want to know?" he moaned hoarsely.

Truly the pirate knew the torture of his own weapon. Wentworth's eyes gleamed. He stepped close. "When do the pirates plan to strike next?" he demanded swiftly.

"In Washington," said Oriano sullenly, "at noon tomorrow."

"But why," Wentworth demanded, "does your gang want the United States involved in a war?"

Oriano twisted his suffering face about, peered at Wentworth out of the corners of puffed, frightened eyes.

"If there was war," he said, "we would have no trouble marketing our goods. No one would ask where they come from. We have nearly a billion dollars' worth of merchandise from steamers."

Wentworth swore softly to himself. Of course, that was it. What a fool he had been not to guess it! Wentworth drew a deep breath. "Where do you strike in Washington?" he asked.

"First at Washington monument," said Oriano dully, "then the Capitol...."

148

But these things were unimportant, Wentworth told himself, impatiently. The big thing was to learn who was the leader of this vast conspiracy. Only by eliminating that man could he end the piracy, check the attack on the nation's capitol.

"Never mind that," he interrupted Oriano's chronicle. "Who is your leader? Who conceived this damnable plot?"

Once more Oriano turned his straining face. There was a sneering smile on it now. "You couldn't figure that out, could you, Spider?" he jeered. "Suppose I don't tell you?"

Wentworth touched Oriano's back with the whip.

"Now—or later, Miguel?"

Oriano threw back his head in a violent physical shudder at the touch of the leather. "I'll talk! I'll talk!" he cried hurriedly. "Our leader is—"

Ram Singh's sudden cry broke in on his words. Wentworth did not turn to see the cause of the alarm. He flung himself flat to the earth, rolling backward frantically. A revolver blasted and two men screamed. One scream was gurgling, the bubbling cry of a strangling man. The other was an expiring groan.

Wentworth staggered to his feet, stared toward Norska. The pilot was sinking to the earth with the Hindu's long-bladed knife buried in his throat. Limply from his hand fell a revolver which somehow had escaped search. Wentworth looked hurriedly at Ram Singh, at Jackson. Neither was hurt. Who then, was that second man who had cried out? Who had breathed an expiring groan?

With a sudden, violent oath, Wentworth whirled toward where Oriano dangled by his hands from the palm-tree. The man's whole body was relaxed; his legs no longer strained to reach the ground. From a round hole in the back of his head, a thin trickle of blood flowed.

Wentworth sprang to his side, but even as he did it, he knew that he was too late, that death had sealed the lips of Oriano even as he was about to reveal the name of the leader—the chief pirate who had plotted to doom a country that he might line his pockets!

Norska had attempted to kill Wentworth and had slain his crony instead.

Wentworth's face became ugly with rage. By heaven, death itself should not stop him now! He plunged toward the plane. He stumbled in the sands and would have fallen but for the ready support of Jackson.

"To Washington," he gasped. "For God's sake, Jackson, get there in time!"

CHAPTER 15
ON TO WASHINGTON!

THE MOMENT the plane gathered enough speed and altitude to make operation of its radio possible, Wentworth began calling New York. At last he got Stanley Kirkpatrick, Commissioner of Police.

"Imperative that all possible army and navy planes be massed at Washington at once," he tapped out the words. "They should be prepared for warfare. Not later than noon. Cannot give reasons now. Fate of nation hinges on this."

He signed that message simply "Dick." Half an hour later as the plane bored into the north toward Washington, the reply came back: "Working on it, but is difficult without explanations. Suggest you rush same soonest. Best of luck. Kirk."

Wentworth read the message grimly. God knew it would be difficult, and yet he could not explain before the fateful hour when the pirate ships boomed above the horizon and sped on the Capitol with their loads of death. This conspiracy was wide-flung. There might be high officials who were involved. The slightest leak and the pirates might strike beforehand. That would lay the country at the mercy of the plotters, and make the declaration of war certain.

He sent one more message, telling Nita to meet him in Washington. Then he left the wireless-key and the cockpit where Jackson was draining every atom of the plane's power in the frantic dash for the Capitol. Ram Singh was at Wentworth's side immediately, offering food. He accepted it absently, frowning on the blackening landscape. It would be well on in the morning before they reached Washington.

The girl, Carmencita, came to where he sat, sank into a chair opposite. Her great dark eyes were glowing with a strange fire.

"It is a pity that Miguel died so soon."

Wentworth looked at her somber-eyed and recalled what Haillie had said of the girl's "appetite for blood." He wondered why any man should find that an attractive trait.

"Yes," he agreed. "Do you know where to reach your father in Washington?"

Nita Van Sloan

The girl answered surprisingly: "He has a suite at the *Ambassador* with Scott Haillie. They're looking for D'Enry."

The statement amazed Wentworth. Haillie and the Don apparently were fierce enemies. The *hidalgo's* son had been killed while returning from a duel with the younger man, yet they had joined forces to hunt D'Enry! Truly, Haillie played his cards well. He deserved to win the girl.

Wentworth's head sagged over his food. His exhausted body demanded rest. He stretched out upon a bench seat and, within minutes, was asleep.

The broken rhythm of slowing motors awoke him and he sat

up to find the plane slanting down to Hoover Field at Washington. He glanced at the clock in the cabin wall! Five o'clock. In seven hours, the bomb planes of the pirates would strike. He did not know where they were hidden—he did not know their leader.

Wentworth got heavily to his feet, stripped off the disguise of Don Estéban, and when he descended from the plane it was in his true identity. He went directly to a phone booth, called Kirkpatrick.

The Commissioner confirmed his fears. "The government wouldn't do a thing about guarding Washington," he said. "I couldn't convince them that the situation was more urgent than protecting the West Coast."

Wentworth cursed vehemently. "I was afraid of that, Kirk. No, there's nothing more you can do. Thanks."

HE HUNG up slowly, stood staring at the phone. He walked heavily out of the booth, met the inquiring gaze of Carmencita, the respectful anxiety of Ram Singh and Jackson. He vouchsafed no information, but told Jackson to stay at the field and keep the plane ready. He directed the Hindu to find a taxi so that they

Ram Singh · · · Jackson

might proceed at once to the Ambassador Hotel where Don Estéban and Haillie were staying.

While the car sped along the roads toward the city, Wentworth sat staring straight ahead at the white wash of headlights on the asphalt. They were rounding the corner from Fourteenth Street and swerving to the curb before the *Ambassador* before the worried set of his lips gave way to a slight, small smile. He had had no plan when he summoned Nita to Washington, had merely been rallying all possible forces for the defense, but now....

"Don't get out, *Señorita,*" he said abrupt. "The information I received over the telephone indicates the same group that killed your brother will attempt to murder you. I want you to go with my servant, Ram Singh, and remain in seclusion until I notify you that it is safe to venture out. It would be better if you did not even communicate with your father, since the assassins might trace you in that way."

"But, *Señor* Wentworth, I do not understand..." she began.

"I don't either, fully," he said, "but you know that Miguel Oriano's associates will stop at nothing. They were the ones who killed your brother, and they want to wipe out your entire family. I am going to warn your father."

For a long minute the girl stared steadily into Wentworth's gray blue eyes, then she nodded slowly. "I must trust you," she said. "How long shall I continue in hiding?"

"Seven hours," he said curtly, then turned to Ram Singh. In rapid, staccato Hindustani, he instructed the Hindu to take

154

the girl to the James Hotel, to keep her isolated there. Then he alighted and entered the *Ambassador.*

He found a note from Nita when he registered and he called her from his room.

"Put on a simple black dress," he told her. "You're in mourning. Fix your hair the way Carmencita wore it that night at the *St. Delroy,* then come to Room 751."

The rigid set of his face relaxed slightly. "Of course, I'm all right, darling. The trip south was... quite successful."

In less than ten minutes, Nita tapped at his door and entered. She found Wentworth perilously garbed; he wore the long black cape, the slouch hat of Tito Caliepi whom all the world knew was the Spider. So that no one could miss his identity, he wore upon the second finger of his right hand, the red-sealed ring of the Spider.

Nita saw these things in a glance as her arms went about his neck. Wentworth smiled, chiding her gently: "What would the house detective think, dearest?"

Nita laughed from sheer relief. "Thank goodness, Dick," she said. "Things can't be so bad as Kirkpatrick indicated, if you can joke."

Wentworth shook his head without answering, seated her beneath strong lights and with skillful hands transformed her sweet face into the countenance of another. He brushed her hair with black powder.

"You are Carmencita de Cinquado y Janández, my love," he told her as he worked. "You left your island home with *Señor* Wentworth whom that terrible Miguel Oriano was about to kill.

155

He is a beast, that Miguel. He had designs upon you and only the loyalty of your brave peons kept him away...."

NITA LISTENED with eyes intent on Wentworth's face while he told her all that had happened on the island and afterward, of the death of Miguel Oriano, and of Wentworth's message to Kirkpatrick to have planes guarding the city.

"You must make it appear, darling," he said, "that you are a dutiful daughter reporting everything to papa. You will say that from what you heard it will not be possible for the army planes to get here before noon, but that they will be here then. Do not worry, sweetheart, but..." He hesitated. So much depended on Nita's perfect conduct of the part, on the success of her deception. Did he dare to tell her how important it was? He shaped her lips finally with touches of a rouge stick, kissed them lightly, then dropped bella donna into her eyes to widen and darken them.

His voice grew suddenly harsh: "My life and the country depend on your success!"

Nita started at the tension in his voice, at the glint in his eyes. Her white hand lifted to his arm. "Is it... as bad as that?" she asked softly.

Wentworth's lips, the thin bloodless lips of Tito Caliepi, twisted wryly. "I'm sorry if I startled you, dear," he said slowly, "but it is as bad as that. Unless our little plan succeeds, I shall have to resort to the torture of men who may be innocent to learn what I have to learn." His fists knotted, his eyes became steely flames. "But I will do even that if it is necessary!"

Nita's fingers wound about his hand; her eyes peered deeply

into his. Outside this door, death might lurk for them both. His sharp scythe might reach for one of them before their eyes met again. Nita sucked in a long, deep breath. Wentworth caught her tightly in his arms.

"*Mañana, señorita,*" he said. "Until tomorrow."

"*Hasta luego, señor,*" she murmured. "Until we meet."

Wentworth closed the door softly on Nita's exit and the grimness returned to his face. It might have been possible to use Carmencita for this task, but he was uncertain of her loyalties. In addition to that, he might be using her to betray her own father, and that was a thing Wentworth would be unwilling to do. No, it was necessary that Nita enact the masquerade. If she remembered that she was not too allow too close scrutiny of her eyes....

Wentworth moved rapidly across to the windows. The suite of Don Estéban was a story below his own, though about fifty feet to the south. Gaining the *hidalgo's* rooms would have been no great feat for the Spider in his full strength, but to a man worn by weeks in the hospital and constant action, it was a considerable task. However, it must be done. His entrance to the suite must be secret.

Swiftly, Wentworth strung out the skeins of the marvelous silken rope which the police had dubbed his "web." Using that as a safety belt, he climbed laboriously to the narrow ledges that girdled the building and inched his way along.

Nerve and strong fingers were the sole requirements of success, but it seemed hours to Wentworth before he reached his goal, and clinging to the awning rods, peeped into an open window of Don Estéban's suite. Luckily, the room was empty.

Pulling in the silken rope which he had doubled over a steam radiator without tying, he eased into the apartment.

From the next room where lights glowed yellowly, he heard the eager rush of Nita's perfect Spanish, the deep-toned interpolations of Don Estéban. So far, apparently, the masquerade was succeeding. Wentworth peered about him in the half dark. HE WAS in a bedroom. He saw that the covers had been thrown back violently and in haste, spotted clothing hung neatly on a closet door. He made a hurried search, found passport papers and held them to the window light. *Remarque D'Enry!* Good God! Here was all the proof that was needed of Don Estéban's connection with the pirates!

Hurriedly, the Spider replaced the papers in the clothing and stole to the doorway. A draped portière half covered it and he peered behind it into the next room. Nita had completed her story and sat upon a davenport staring at D'Enry, grotesque in a lounge-robe two sizes too large for him.

"*Señor* Wentworth said that you killed my brother," she told him directly.

D'Enry laughed sharply. His hands flew in an excited gesture. "It was *Señor* Wentworth himself who committed the murder," he said vehemently. "Do you think that if I had done this thing these two gentlemen would permit me to remain at large?" His flying hands indicated Haillie and Don Estéban, who stood somberly gazing at the woman they believed to be Carmencita.

Haillie stood with both hands rammed into the pockets of his dressing robe. "D'Enry is convinced that Wentworth and this criminal called the Spider are one and the same man," he explained slowly. "He has proved to us very convincingly that the Spider committed the murder. I think that before we take any action in the matter, we ought to call on Wentworth and see what he has to say."

"*Sí,*" said Don Estéban slowly. "That would be excellent. I prefer that he should answer to me rather than to the police." There was a world of bitter hatred in his words. "I think we shall call at once on this *Señor* Wentworth who so cleverly impersonated me."

Wentworth was frowning. This was not at all the type of reaction he had expected from these men. His hand slid to the automatic beneath his arm, slipped it from its holster. He stepped clear of the doorway.

"Raise your hands, gentlemen," he ordered suavely.

Nita choked down a scream. It was cleverly done, an outcry that would not carry beyond the door. The three men whirled and D'Enry's hand darted toward his dressing robe pocket. The black muzzle of Wentworth's gun stared him in the face and the hand hesitated, then lifted slowly. Only Don Estéban failed to raise his hands as ordered. He stood rigid with indignation, staring at the hunchbacked figure with its draped cloak.

"The Spider!" stammered D'Enry. "The Spider. This is the man, Don Estéban. He is the one who murdered André!"

The bloodless lips of the Spider stirred slightly. It might have been a smile.

"Sorry, but I must disclaim the honor, D'Enry," he said gently. "I heard what you had been saying about me and that is why I came tonight."

His eyes sought out the stern face of Don Estéban. *"Señor,"* he said, "anyone you ask among the police will tell you that the Spider always prints his seal upon those he kills. If they are fair, they will tell you also that he kills only to avert greater crimes." His eyes returned to D'Enry and there was a brilliant hate in their depths. "What is your evidence, pig?"

The Frenchman sneered, and Wentworth spoke sharply to Nita. *"Señorita,* you will please remain seated. I should not wish to harm a woman."

"I thought," D'Enry jeered, "that you killed only criminals."

Wentworth nodded. "That is true. I have just heard Carmencita warn her father that the pirates had better come earlier than noon, or their plans will be defeated. I think I am justified in classing her and the rest of you as, at the very least, criminals. I am glad to learn of the work of that clever chap, Wentworth. It is always a race to see which of us will triumph over the enemy first. This time, I shall be glad to assist him. I think it is my duty to see that none of you carries word of this warning to the pirates." His voice sharpened suddenly. "Face the wall, all of you!"

DON ESTÉBAN spluttered in angry protest. For a moment it seemed to Wentworth that he would fly at him but in the end, he too turned to the wall. With swift facility, the Spider knotted ropes about the wrists of the men, bound them tightly. He had just rigged the last gag when Nita ran suddenly for the door. With a curse, Wentworth hurled himself after her, yanking loose the telephone as he bolted past. He plunged out just behind her, clapped the door shut. Nita turned toward him with anxious eyes. He nodded toward a bend of the hall. They hurried there and descended toward the first floor.

As they went, Wentworth stripped off his disguise. He wore a suit under the cape and when the cloak was draped over his arm, the slouch of the black hat shaped more stylishly and the hunch gone from his back, there was little to identify him with the twisted menace of the Spider.

"I smashed the telephone in the room," he told her. "When those three get loose, at least one of them will go to send a warning to the pirates. I hope by that means to discover both who the leader is and the whereabouts of the planes that they are sending to bomb Washington."

Nita smiled quickly up at him. "It's a good plan, Dick," she said quietly. "If I did my part well, it should work."

Wentworth was frowning slightly. "I think you did well," he said. "I heard almost all your story. The only thing that worries me was the necessity for your leaving when I did. I am going to try to cover that by sending a message to the room saying that I am holding you hostage to make sure that none of them warns the Pirates. I think it unlikely they will go to the police about it." His frown changed to a tight smile. He left Nita before they came to the desk, dashed off the note in crudely drawn capital letters, instructing the clerk that it should be slid at once beneath the door of Don Estéban's suite.

"I don't want to disturb him," he said, "but I think it is important that he get this the first moment he awakens."

The clerk, pocketing a five-dollar bill, thought so too, and

Wentworth rejoined Nita. The two of them entered a car which Wentworth had hired by phone and there they waited.

"I am acquiring a growing respect for D'Enry," Wentworth admitted. "At first, I did not believe him capable of being the brains of this pirate crew, but now I am no longer sure. It may be that he has deceived Don Estéban…" He cut off sharply, leaning forward to stare at the door of the *Ambassador*.

Although it had been less than ten minutes since he had left the apartment of Don Estéban, there were the three men he had left securely bound there, walking together out of the door of the hotel! The sight drew an amazed exclamation from. Nita, too. She knew how well Wentworth bound his prisoners, knew that it would be practically impossible for the men to escape so swiftly without outside assistance.

"It's possible," Wentworth muttered, "that the bellhop who carried the note went inside."

But even as he said that, he knew the boy could not have summoned help from below, opened the door, and freed the men in this short while. His thoughts flew back to a scene on the cabin in the Hudson just before he had been shot. D'Enry, securely bound moments before, was standing in the doorway with a gun in his hand. Wentworth shook his head sharply. Even the Spider, with all his skill, could not escape so quickly from ropes. There was some clever trick that D'Enry knew.

Wentworth had touched the motor of his car to life and now, as the three men entered a taxi and sped off, he meshed the gears and slid forward in pursuit. After a few blocks farther on, the cab stopped and D'Enry entered an all-night garage.

Wentworth slid out quickly from behind the wheel. "Follow Don Estéban, darling," he said. "You can reach me by leaving word at the *Ambassador*. I'll follow D'Enry."

He darted to the shadows in the walk without waiting for a reply, and when the taxi ahead got under way again, Nita drove in its wake. Wentworth looked swiftly about him. It was a neighborhood of garages such as spring up on the fringes of wealthy residential areas. He had little trouble in renting another car. When D'Enry finally drove out in a low-built, new Stutz speedster, Wentworth swung from the curb in pursuit.

For two hours, while day came grayly again in the east and turned into a red-rayed sun, he followed while the Frenchman swung westward from the Baltimore road, bored on into the outlying hills of the Alleghenies. Wentworth's jubilation mounted steadily. He was positive now that success was crowning his efforts at last. He need only trail D'Enry to the airport, summon police to smash him and his men and the battle would be won!

Suddenly, without warning, a double blast rocked Wentworth's car. The shot of a rifle was echoed by the hissing explosion as the right front tire blew out. The Lincoln rocked wildly, lunging toward the ditch while Wentworth fought the steering wheel.

Even while he battled to hold the car to the road he saw a half dozen men burst from the thickets on either flank, saw the glint of guns in their hands and knew that he had driven into a Pirate trap!

163

CHAPTER 16
THE PIRATE SQUADRON

WENTWORTH KNEW that there was no chance of escape. Through the leafless boughs of trees, he caught the gleam of three automobiles parked on masked woods trails. Ahead, D'Enry had flung his Stutz across the road and waited with an automatic in his hand. With sound tires, there might have been a chance of smashing aside the leader's roadster and racing to safety. Even with the right front tire sending thumping shudders through the whole frame…?

The Spider shook his head. Escape might save his own life, but it would not defeat the pirates. It was obvious that someone other than D'Enry had flashed a warning ahead and set this trap. That meant another leader in Washington. Wentworth knew that the men did not intend his immediate death or the hail of lead would have swept his car instead of merely blowing out a tire.

With stabbing motions of his foot, he braked the Lincoln to a rocking halt. He had made a deliberate choice, a gamble of his life for the safety of his country. If he dashed on, he might escape death, but he would lose the trail and be able to do nothing to save Washington and smash the pirate gang. If he stayed, he would at least learn the whereabouts of the pirate headquarters. What followed then would depend on his own swift wits—and the length of time the pirates allowed him to live.

Men swarmed to the running board, snatched his guns roughly from their holsters. D'Enry, smiling afar, called an order and they jerked him from his seat, carried him to one of their own cars. Wentworth heard his own car start, heard its motor roar up, then a terrific smashing concussion jerked his head about. The Lincoln was piled up in the ditch and already flames were licking over the wreckage.

D'Enry waved a mocking salute and trailed the line of cars in a high-speed dash across country. It was a half hour later that the Stutz spun from the main road into a narrower highway. Three miles of that and there was another turn onto a lane that made the driver of Wentworth's car curse and jounce the occupants ludicrously upon the deep cushions.

The Spider knew that they must be within a very short distance now of the field where the pirate bombers waited. He knew that once he reached the airport he would be under a heavy, perpetually-watchful guard. His death might be scheduled for the instant of arrival, a victory to bolster the courage of the renegade pilots who would attack the Capitol.

The car topped a sharp rise, slanted downward where rain ruts made the road all but impassable. Despite their crawling pace, the jouncing lurch of the machine increased. The two guards who sat to either side of Wentworth were clinging to the sides and attempting at the same time to keep him covered with their guns.

The Spider bided his time, floundering about loosely in his seat, cursing as violently as the others. The car gave a particularly heavy lurch and he flounced upon the man to his right. At the same instant, he lifted his feet, kicked the guard on his left violently on the shins. The man's cry of pain echoed the alarm of the man Wentworth had seized. Before he could strike, he had snatched the automatic, smashed it against the man's skull.

The driver slammed on brakes, clawed for a gun that lay on the seat at his side. The man at Wentworth's left already had his weapon in hand. There was no time to strike him. The Spider's captured weapon spat once and the bullet, at almost contact range, smashed the man violently back into his corner.

A savage chop with the barrel of the automatic and the driver's right wrist cracked; the gun dropped from his hand. His howl of pain mingled with fear as the Spider's automatic centered on his forehead.

"Drive on," said Wentworth grimly. "That wrist will probably pain you, but not so much, I should think, as a bullet through the head!"

The driver blinked, his face still distorted with pain and fear. Then the Spider's words penetrated. He grasped at the chance of reprieve, sent the car plunging down grade, bouncing and swaying wildly. Wentworth braced himself with his legs stiffly against the back of the front seat and hung on.

With a roar, the car burst wildly out from the narrow lane onto a grassy field. Wentworth flung a swift glance about. All around the level green were hangars masked by trees. They were filled with huge bombing planes which stood nose out, ready to go to the line. Three planes were in the open, their motors turning over idly. They were small pursuit jobs and the muzzles of machine-guns caught the light on their noses.

With a jab of his automatic, Wentworth sped the driver toward those three planes. Twenty feet away, the man snatched at the brake, sprawled from the car and ran in screaming erratic flight toward the woods.

"The Spider!" he screamed. "The Spider! Kill the Spider!"

WENTWORTH SPRANG from the car, jerked it into low gear and sent it trundling toward the nearest of the three pursuit planes. He darted for the ship at the other end of the line. From the far edge of the field, where the road debouched, he heard the rattle of gunfire above the muttering of idling engines. Men darted from hangars with drawn pistols in their hands.

He saw the guns of the men from the hangars swivel toward him while he was still yards from the plane he had chosen. Then a rending, crashing explosion tore the air. The car had rammed nose-on into the whirling propeller of one of the pursuit ships!

With a snarling roar, the propeller tore into the welded steel top of the car, snapped off short. The ship reared up on its tail like a frightened horse and its motor bellowed and quivered as the unbalanced crankshaft, wrenched by the smash of the propeller, racked its frame.

Wentworth scrambled to the plane at the far end of the line while the crackup distracted the gunmen. As his hand snatched at the throttle and jerked it wide, the wrecked plane lifted straight up on the nose of the still laboring car, teetered over and crashed on its sister.

Wentworth's ship leaped forward under the impetus of the gun, skimmed the ground into the push of the wind. The chattering burst of a machine-gun vibrated somewhere ahead. Its stuttering challenge was faintly audible through the roar of the

Wentworth nosed down. The men on the field ran—but few

ran far. Machine-guns were chattering from the air.

engine—then that and all other sounds was drowned out in an explosion behind.

Wentworth's ship had been easing from the earth under his skillful hand, but that ripping blast battered it down again. It bounded wildly, the tail wrenched to the right, swung about to the left, then she soared nose-up for fifty feet, hanging on the propeller. Only Wentworth's marvelous hand saved him from death then. He kept the motor gunning full strength, and instead of waiting for the ship to stall, threw her with the torque of her motor into a steep bank the instant she was slipping off to crash.

For a heart-beat, the plane hovered on the brink of destruction, then Wentworth's jockeying won and she screamed into a short dive, zoomed and leaped above the trees that fringed the field. The ship was in complete control again now and answering a firm hand, swung in a vertical bank about the field.

Where the two other planes had stood on the line, there remained only a flaming pile of wreckage. Spattered small fires burned on all sides where blazing gasoline had been hurled. A group of men was fighting furiously to save a hangar from the licking hot tongues. Grim laughter broke from the Spider.

He nosed down, pressed hard on the thumb trips of the twin machine-guns nested in the cowling. Gray-smoking tracers belched from the muzzles, dug up the earth before the hangar, and as Wentworth tugged on the stick, bullets swept across the five men who battled the fire.

There was no need to wait for the results of that swift blow—no need to see the men crumple brokenly to earth and unchecked flames leap higher. The plane swept out of its zoom and upward in a loop that turned into an Immelmann. Back down the length of the field Wentworth shot. Two more automobiles had run out of the woods now. Men were scattered on all sides of them, firing upward in his path.

Wentworth nosed down. The men ran, but few ran far. Machine-guns were chattering again from the air. The Spider's eyes were gleaming. In that last burst of bullets he had seen a strange thing. He had seen patches of flame leap up among the grass where his bullets struck. And he knew what that meant. The belts of his machine-guns carried inflammable bullets! A fiendish weapon that the pirates had planned to use against army planes that might bar their path. One of those bullets through a gasoline task and a pilot died in screaming torture. Well, the Spider had another use for them.

Shooting upward in another zoom, spiraling once to gain altitude, he swept downward again. This time he fired not at men but at the tree-masked hangars. Down one side of the field he swept, then up the other with his machine-guns blasting fiery death upon the bomb-laden ships.

WHEN NEXT he swung aloft to look down upon his handiwork, three more hangars were swept by flames. Men were striving frantically to drag bombers clear of leaping red tongues of death. A bomber, wheeled out into the open, already was ablaze.

Without warning, the plane flew to pieces, belching smoke and yellow-tipped flame high into the air. The fire had found a bomb. Of the men who had fought to save her, not a trace remained. But other ships had escaped the bath of fire; their motors were roaring for the take-off. Again and again Wentworth swooped on that field of death and his fiery bullets played havoc.

Only one bomber finally got into the air and Wentworth harried it over the tree-tops, sweeping it with his deadly lead—the incendiary bullets—from end to end, dodging the outreaching fingers of the tracers that answered. Abruptly the black puff of smoke, the belch of red flame that heralded victory—and death—burst out from the other plane's nose and Wentworth wheeled into a looping, stunting whirl of final victory.

Suddenly, without warning, the instrument board shattered before his eyes. Hot oil spurted into his face. He did not need to turn his head, did not need to look for the gray smoke of tracers to know what had happened. While he had harried that one bomber which he had thought the last on the field, another craft had taken wing and was on his tail!

As the ship sped past, Wentworth twisted his head for a glimpse of the killer who had so nearly finished the Spider. He caught sight of a small smiling face, a mustached goggleless man in a pursuit ship that matched his own.

It was Remarque D'Enry....

From one of the hangars, the Frenchman had snatched a plane and soared under cover of the attack on the bombers to duel the Spider to the death in the skies!

In that single glance, Wentworth saw something else, too. He saw that the Frenchman handled the ship like a veteran, for sharply as the Spider had dodged, deft as had been his maneuver, the pirate plane was still behind him, mounting again for a death-dealing dive upon his tail!

For minutes, the two ships whirled and shrieked in a savage battle without gaining advantage, without either reaching a position where he could pour lead into the vitals of his enemy. Once Wentworth's bullets raked the side of D'Enry's fuselage, but before the fatal black punctures could reach the spot where the Frenchman sat, the ship had dodged out of the way. Once the gray tracers of the Pirate streaked past Wentworth's ears and sent splinters of hot lead into his face.

After that exchange, Wentworth fenced more warily. For minutes the love of battle, the intoxication of victory had swept him into the fight, but now his head was clearing. He thought back to that ambush on the road and recalled his flash of knowledge that someone back in Washington had phoned word ahead to plant the trap. That meant that even if he smashed D'Enry, another leader of the Pirates would remain to harry mankind, to loose the fearful lightning of bombs on Washington.

He could not afford to kill D'Enry!

WENTWORTH'S HANDS moved in answer to his thought. As the Frenchman slashed past in another futile, bullet-roaring dive, he sent his own plane into a steep climb. He knew that D'Enry could do no more than match his rise, could not overtake him, for they operated the same kind of planes. Together, he and D'Enry reached for the ceiling, but the Frenchman could not gain an advantage and Wentworth did not want one.

It was over an emergency field in Maryland, near the border

of the District of Columbia, that Wentworth threw his plane into a screaming power-dive. His maneuver had taken D'Enry by surprise and the Frenchman trailed from the start. Staring backward, the Spider saw the flicker of powder-flame through the whirling propeller, but he did not even bother to kick the rudder. The Frenchman was too far away.

Downward, ever downward, the two planes plunged. They had been racing at better than fifteen thousand feet and they dropped to less than five thousand before Wentworth threw his speedy ship into the maneuver which he had been planning. First he slowed his dive until the hopeful Frenchman had narrowed the distance between them almost to effective gun range, then he ruddered out of his dive and spun upward. So great was D'Enry's speed that he dared not zoom out of his dive.

He fought to flatten out—and then the Spider was on his tail!

Wentworth burned the air blue around the Frenchman's plane. He never quite hit the pirate ship, but he never allowed D'Enry an instant's respite from the shrilling bullets. Above and to both sides, the lead whined and only in descent was there safety. When the pirate dropped, Wentworth cut his guns. The instant the ship nosed up, lead shrieked again. Finally the Frenchman took the hint and shot toward the earth.

Wentworth waited until the pirate's wheels touched the ground, until he actually sprang from his ship, before he came rocketing to earth. D'Enry already was racing for the woods that skirted the field, was within fifty feet of them when the Spider shot his plane into a wild sideslip, yanked out of it and stopped with a twenty-foot roll directly between the man and the woods.

He kept his motor roaring, ruddered the nose around and bored down on the Frenchman. D'Enry flung his automatic and emptied it at the plane. His bullets clanged on the propeller, thudded into the engine-block without serious damage, and the ship trundled swiftly on. The pirate threw down his gun, threw up his hands.

Wentworth swung his ship broadside, skidded to a halt within ten feet of the Pirate. He covered him with an automatic. The small smile was gone from D'Enry's face now. It was haggard with fear, twisted with rage.

"You've got me," he shouted as Wentworth leaped to the ground with ready gun, "but you can't save Washington!"

It was the taunt of a beaten man, but the Spider knew instantly that it was more than that. D'Enry meant that—even as Wentworth had suspected—the plans would go forward even without the planes, even without himself. He meant that the Pirates would sweep on to the victory that meant plunging the United States into ruinous warfare!

Even while the man spoke, Pirates might be striking in Washington! Wentworth reached out with his gun and D'Enry toppled unconscious to the ground. Swift as light were the movements of Wentworth's hands as he bound the Frenchman. He tossed him athwart the wing of his ship, bound him there and sprang to the cockpit.

Ten minutes later, he set the ship down on Hoover Field, unbound the still unconscious D'Enry and signaled for an ambulance. The crash wagon raced toward him, the stretcher-bearers flung the Frenchman in, sprang to the step on the

175

rear. Wentworth jumped in beside the driver, and the man's eyes widened as a gun dug into his ribs.

"We aren't stopping at your hospital," said Wentworth. "We're going straight to the city. Savvy?"

The driver's face was pale. "I savvy!" he said and slammed the ambulance toward a closed gate in the frail fence that bordered the field. He didn't wait for the gate to be opened. The ambulance scarcely hesitated as it smashed the white palings to splinters, skidded with shrieking tires on the concrete road beyond, slithered and darted for the city.

IN THAT soaring flight, Wentworth had had time enough to plan. In the ten minutes that had passed since D'Enry had voiced the taunt he had had time to fit that into his plans too. He knew of only two means by which the pirates could precipitate war. There would have to be a spectacular assassination, or a bombing—and the pirates inclined to bombing. An assassination might prove difficult.

While the ambulance roared along the road, siren going full blast, Wentworth leaned close to the driver.

"Listen," he said. "I used the gun because there was no time to argue. I'm a secret service man and this prisoner of mine has been plotting to bomb the city. He told me just before I knocked him out that the bombs are still going to go off. I want you to high-tail it for the Ambassador Hotel. I'm going back and talk with this baby!"

The driver could not take his eyes off the road. "That's okay by me. You can count on me."

Wentworth scrambled to the rear. The stretcher bearers, white-faced and angry, had climbed inside. Wentworth shouted the same story at them while he worked over D'Enry. The Frenchman came around under his ministrations.

"Listen," one of the stretcher men was yelling in Wentworth's ear. "We're going to have trouble getting through to the *Ambassador*. Since morning the town's been crazy. They heard the town was going to be bombed by them damned Easterners and the mob is packed all the way along Pennsylvania Avenue. They called out the troops to drive people out of the Capitol. They want war, and they ought to have it."

D'Enry's eyes were beginning to focus now and Wentworth glared down at him. His mind was speeding back over his battles with the Pirates. What was it that Miguel Oriano had said just before he died? Yes, that was it! The bombing of Washington monument was to be the signal. Wentworth bent over D'Enry.

"I'm taking you to Washington monument," he shouted in the Pirate's ear. "Then the first bomb will keep you from enjoying the rest of them."

The Frenchman was on the edge of consciousness, did not have full control over his facial expression. He could not conceal the stark fear that Wentworth's words had caused.

The Spider straightened with a jerk. "What time is it?" he bellowed.

The stretcher-bearer slid a bony wrist out of a white sleeve. The watch's hands stood at a quarter past eleven. Would the pirates wait for twelve o'clock, the hour the Congress met, to strike? Wentworth hoped frantically that they would. On that one hope depended all his plans, all his chances of smashing

177

once and for all the Pirates' grip upon America. He scrambled forward.

"Listen," he yelled at the driver, "I've got to make the *Ambassador* in five minutes. I don't give a damn if you have to plough through an army to get there."

Wentworth saw that the speedometer needle wavered at seventy-three. The driver did not take his eyes off the road. He screwed his mouth around on the side and said one word:

"Okay!"

Even as he spoke, two men in khaki leaped into the road with rifles on whose muzzles bayonets gleamed. They jerked their rifles to their shoulders.

CHAPTER 17
WASHINGTON MONUMENT

WENTWORTH'S HAND hovered on the butt of his automatic. Never in his life had he struck down an agent of law and order, whether that man was a policeman or a soldier. But these soldiers stood between the nation and its salvation. Minutes were hostages given to the enemy.

Even as Wentworth hesitated, the ambulance driver's foot kicked a button on the floor. A gong like the clap of doom bonged out. In the same instant the siren squawled. Years-old habit actuated the soldiers. They leaped at the sound. Their bullets went wild—and the ambulance was streaking on down the road, rounding a curve on smoking tires, rocking on into the straightaway.

"Good boy!" Wentworth yelled at the driver.

He saw the man's ears move in a wide grin. "I said 'Okay!' didn't I?" was his only response.

The city limits leaped toward them. Fourteenth Street skimmed beneath their tires and the marching mobs of Pennsylvania Avenue sprang in sight. Once more the placards demanding war flaunted before Wentworth's eyes. The ambulance roared on without a second's let-up in speed. The siren shrieked, wailed, screamed out its eerie warning. Men scattered from its path. One man pulled a revolver, stood squarely in its path, then lost his nerve and leaped clear just in time.

The car whirled another corner, skated halfway across the street, then its brakes shrieked and it slid to the curb at the entrance of the *Ambassador*. Wentworth clapped the driver on the shoulder, shoved a wad of bills into his hand. He yanked D'Enry from the back of the ambulance, hustled him toward the door. People stared curiously, but Wentworth had a gun openly in his hand. In their minds, gun and legitimate authority went together. They did not interfere.

Behind him, Wentworth heard the ambulance driver let out a yelp.

"Hey, mister, hey!" he cried. "This is too much! Gawd amighty, a thousand dollars!"

Wentworth punched through a revolving door, went straight across the staring lobby to the elevators. He went to his own room, found Jackson there with Nita, still in her disguise as Carmencita.

"I called Jackson in from the field," she said swiftly, then stopped, staring at D'Enry.

"Good!" snapped Wentworth. "Jackson, take this rat to Washington Monument—the top floor—and tie him up so he can't get away. Then go down to the first floor and don't let anybody enter until I come. You're in your uniform, and a gun at your belt will look like military police to anybody who comes around."

"And Jackson," said Wentworth as the doughty ex-sergeant hustled the Frenchman to the door. "If I'm not there by five minutes of twelve, get as far away from the Monument as possible."

Jackson passed and looked back. He shook D'Enry's shoulder. "What about this guy?"

"Just leave him."

D'Enry's thin squeal was cut off by Jackson's heavy palm across his mouth. The door closed behind them. Wentworth whirled to Nita.

"Haillie and Don Estéban?" he asked.

"Both downstairs in their rooms," Nita said rapidly, recognizing from the urgency of Wentworth's tones the need for haste. "I followed them an hour. They separated once and Don Estéban made some telephone calls while Haillie waited in the car. I couldn't catch the numbers."

"Haillie stayed in the car?" Wentworth snapped. It certainly looked as if Don Estéban had phoned the warning to the Pirate squadron.

Nita nodded. "So far as I know." Her speed and animation seemed odd in her make-up of a languid Mexican girl.

"Okay," said Wentworth. "Now come with me. You're still Carmencita to that bunch downstairs." As they walked rapidly through the corridors down a single flight of stairs, Wentworth outlined the situation. "I just rescued you from the Spider. He was busy somewhere else at the time so we didn't tangle. Tell it anyway you want to, but make it fast."

HIS RAP at the door of Don Estéban's suite was so heavy and imperative that Haillie yanked the door open angrily. His eyes stared wide at sight of Carmencita and Wentworth.

"I found her a prisoner in a deserted house out of Baltimore," Wentworth said swiftly, "while I was chasing these Pirates. She says the Spider had her a prisoner. I'd have liked to wait and meet the man, but there wasn't time." He was inside the apartment now, talking rapidly. "I've found André's murderer," he went on. "I know where he'll be up to twelve o'clock, but after that God knows where he'll be."

"Where is it?" Don Estéban demanded quickly.

His eyes were smoldering. His arm was caressingly about the shoulders of the girl he thought was his daughter.

"Washington Monument," Wentworth said. "Exactly at noon." He glanced at the clock on the table. "In thirty-five minutes."

"Let's go," Haillie said excitedly.

Don Estéban hesitated, his arm still about Nita's shoulders. "Why should he be in such a place at that time?" he growled. "How do you know?"

"*Por Dios!*" Nita cried in her best Spanish. "What do we care

181

how the good God delivers our enemy into our hands, so long as we find him!"

Don Estéban caught the infection of the excitement. He too strode toward the door. "Wait here, Carmencita."

Nita ran after him. *"Por Dios,"* she cried. "Shall I not see my brother avenged?"

Haillie and Don Estéban both tried to dissuade her, but she was obstinate and time was flying. They climbed into a taxi at eleven-thirty precisely. It could not batter through the mob as the ambulance had done. It was compelled to make a wide circle around the White House grounds and approach the Monument from the opposite side. It was a quarter of twelve when they alighted.

Jackson was standing in the doorway on braced feet, his gun swinging at his thigh. It was clear that he had had his difficulties in keeping the Monument clear. As the others entered the base of the tall obelisk that climbs more than five hundred feet straight up into the heavens, Wentworth paused for a moment beside Jackson.

"When the elevator comes back down, take the operator away," he said. "This building is going to blow up in less than fifteen minutes."

The elevator climbed with a smooth regular pace upward. It was not fast. It was not slow, but it took over two minutes to reach the top. As they climbed up the last flight of stairs to the peak, Don Estéban, who had entered the platform first, staggered back.

"D'Enry!" he cried.

Wentworth thrust Don Estéban forward, tossed a loop over Haillie's shoulders and arms, and noosed it tight. He held a gun on Don Estéban while he completed the tying of Haillie.

"Listen," Wentworth whispered in Haillie's ear. "I know D'Enry is one of the Pirates, but I'm not sure of Don Estéban. I want you to listen when I leave. I'll get you clear in time."

He thrust Haillie violently forward, bound Don Estéban and Nita next. Then he stood looking at the trussed foursome. It still lacked ten minutes of twelve.

"One of you is the leader of the Pirates," Wentworth said slowly. "I know D'Enry is one, but you others I am not sure of. This I do know. At twelve exactly, this Monument is to be blown up by one of your bombs. I hope that before that time, one of you will confess and tell me where to find the bomb, otherwise…" He leaned over and looked at Haillie's watch. "It's nine minutes of twelve. D'Enry, you've got your own skin to save. Don Estéban, there are both you and your daughter to consider. Haillie, your beloved and yourself.

"I'm going downstairs a little way for four minutes. Then I'm coming back. At the end of that time, it would be better for the guilty one to talk."

He turned and strode down the steps. At each platform below, there were stone seats set into the walls. These platforms occurred only at the doors of the elevator. The only other thing in the slim tower was the continuous spiral of stairs. Wentworth went down two flights and hid himself in the window-seat niche.

BARELY HAD he concealed himself when he heard the

183

slow, furtive tread of feet upon the stairs above. Once more the Pirate leader had demonstrated his facility in getting out of bonds. But the man was not alone. There was also the tread of a woman's slippers.

"Where is father?"

Wentworth could not hear the muttered answer, but abruptly a man sprang toward the niche and his gun blazed almost directly in Wentworth's face. The Spider had been expecting that. He had allowed his toe tip to protrude from his hiding place deliberately to betray it. But when the man whirled about the corner, Wentworth was not standing. He had been crouched with his knees bent. Now he sprang upward and his fist struck the nerve center of the man's pistol arm. Another blow slammed the man against the elevator cage and there was the metallic clank of handcuffs that snapped him fast to that barrier.

"Hurry back upstairs, dear," said Wentworth to Nita, "and free Don Estéban. I'm afraid you'll find that D'Enry is already dead." As Nita hastened up the stairs, he turned to confront the leader of the Pirates—*Scott Haillie!*

"You see, Haillie," he said. "You didn't wipe the ring quite clean after you cut D'Enry's throat."

Haillie's start of surprise, his glance at his hand shackled to the iron grillwork of the cage were a betrayal in themselves. But the blood was there, discoloring the remarkable diamond ring that Haillie always wore.

"You won't cut through that steel with your ring, Haillie," Wentworth said calmly. "Yes, I guessed what it was. It's a pickpocket's ring, the kind that has a tiny curved blade of razor steel concealed in the part that goes about your finger. It works with a touch on the stone, doesn't it, Haillie?"

Wentworth stepped forward and touched the ring. He barely jumped back in time to escape Haillie's vicious left-handed blow. But Wentworth had achieved his purpose. From the curve of the ring, a steel blade had flashed out.

"With that ring," said Wentworth, "you freed D'Enry of his ropes in that cabin on the river while you pretended to choke and smack him in anger. You cut yourself loose in Don Estéban's room. And just a few minutes ago, you did it again upstairs. I was inclined to suspect Don Estéban because of the island affair. I was prepared, in fact, to see D'Enry and Don Estéban come down the stairs together. The instant I saw you, saw that smear of blood on your ring, I knew—knew you were guilty."

Haillie had been staring at Wentworth with a mixture of fright and pity on his face. "Listen, Wentworth," he broke in finally, "for heaven's sake, don't be a fool, It's true I have the ring, that I cut myself free upstairs with it, but those other things I didn't do. Don't be misled by appearances…."

Wentworth shook his head, smiling. "I'm not," he said. Nita came down the stairs, helping Don Estéban. D'Enry was not with them.

"You were right about D'Enry," Nita said, shuddering as she looked at Haillie.

The cables of the elevator were snaking upward to a faint distant creaking, and as Nita spoke, the cage reached the level on which they stood. Jackson threw open the door and stood aside.

Wentworth nodded, motioned Nita and Don Estéban into

the car. The lean aristocrat seemed dazed, his eyes vacant as they stared at Haillie.

"For God's sake!" cried Haillie. "You aren't going to leave me here?"

"Why not?" shrugged Wentworth, stepping into the car also. "Just use that little ring with which you murdered your companion D'Enry. Possibly, it can cut that handcuff steel also."

"Four and a half minutes of twelve, sir," Jackson reported in the same monotonous voice.

"All right," Wentworth said. "Let's go!"

"For God's sake, wait!" Haillie screamed. "I'll tell you where it is!"

"Talk fast!" Wentworth snarled at him.

"It's in the base of the elevator shaft—a small one wedged under the pulley block. There are seven others in the walls with percussion caps."

"Down!" Wentworth barked.

"Four minutes of twelve, sir," Jackson said. "We'll reach the bottom with about a minute and a half to spare."

Wentworth nodded. He was watching the slow upward slide of floors past the door of the cage.

"When we reach the bottom, Jackson," he said. "Take Miss Nita and this gentleman away from here as fast as you can. I'll get the bomb."

"No, Dick!" Nita cried. Her voice sounded smothered. Don Estéban turned his head slowly, looked at her.

Wentworth shrugged. "There is no sense in risking more than one life," he said quietly. "There's a chance Haillie lied about the location of the bomb, or that his men did not place it where he told them."

"I would never have suspected him," Don Estéban said dully.

Wentworth shook his head. "It took me a long time to get around to it," he confessed. "Especially after D'Enry tried to kill your son at the Dueling Rocks and Haillie apparently helped me out. I know now that he staged an escape from D'Enry only to make sure that I would walk into a trap that he prepared for me. It was probably Haillie who killed your son, throwing his body overboard from my launch. He undoubtedly lied about putting André into a taxi after they reached shore.

"I don't know whether his love for your daughter was real or pretended, but it's not to be doubted that he wanted your island. Probably he planned at first to gain it by marriage. Later, when he found that was impossible, he staged that duel to make a breach between you and himself. It was his purpose then to make it impossible for anyone to attach to himself any suspicion that might rise from your connection with the island headquarters of the gang."

"Two minutes of twelve, sir," Jackson said in the same dead voice.

Despite Wentworth's quiet talk, he was tense with the desire for action. If that bomb exploded before he could reach it, his death was not the only thing that would result. There would be no one to tell the nation how mistaken it had been in its attempts to force a war upon a peaceful nation. No one—because it was unlikely that in a minute and a half, Nita and Jackson and Don Estéban could get far enough away to save themselves.

The explosion of the bomb would also destroy a shrine of the nation. It would be taken as a final insult. Undoubtedly there were still minor leaders of the Pirates scattered about among the mobs who would make capital of it, never knowing that the leaders were dead.

Wentworth shook his head. He must reach the bomb in time. "You probably don't know of the attempt to assassinate André during the duel. I think Haillie had that arranged, too, intending to weaken you by your son's death and dispose of me by having me accused of the crime. I think, too, that he feared to face your son's sword."

They were almost to the bottom now. Wentworth tensed his muscles for the dash down the flight of concrete steps to the basement, the scramble for the bomb.

"Haillie's family always have had the power of wealth," he said, speaking hurriedly. If Don Estéban and Nita could get clear, he wanted them to be able to tell the whole story. "Haillie never had a great many scruples about how he won anything. There were a great many who considered his tactics in fencing unethical in the extreme. It's queer how a man will show up on the fencing mat...."

"Haillie had wealth long enough to get the love of power. When his family lost the money, he sought to regain it. I imagine that D'Enry, whom Haillie met in the Montmartre, was responsible for suggesting the ways and means of doing it. Miguel Oriano was just a tool...."

"One and a half minutes of twelve, sir," said Jackson. But despite his efforts at calmness, his voice sounded tight and strained. "Here we are!" He seized the door and wrenched it open.

"Get out of here fast!"

Already he was at the head of the concrete steps. He went down them in a single leap, doubled forward to clear the heading. He struck the bottom, went down on hands and knees, but was up immediately, slamming around the elevator pit to the front.

Upstairs he heard the swift tap-tap of feet, heard Jackson protest, heard Nita's imperious voice. Distantly the screaming of Haillie still echoed, but abruptly that ceased. The pulley blocks that hid the bomb where were they? Wentworth fought his racing heart to quietness, fought to still the whirring of blood in his ears.

There were the pulley blocks. He reached them in a bound. But there were four of them! He scooped his hands under the first. Nothing there. He sprang to the second.

"One minute to twelve," said a quiet voice behind him, the voice of Nita! Wentworth's heart gave a great bound within him, but he did not even turn his head. The third pulley block had revealed nothing also. He flung himself desperately at the fourth. Death was very near. The grim skeleton's scythe was drawn back for the stroke, but Wentworth's heart was glad within him. If he had to die, this was how they had always wished it, he and Nita, side by side.

He scooped under the fourth pulley block and his hands met beneath it.

The bomb was not there!

189

"Half a minute of twelve," said Nita. She tried to keep her voice calm, but in spite of herself, it broke slightly. Wentworth heard her feet move swiftly toward him. Side by side when the moment came. Nita's feet were quick and sharp as clock ticks.

"Stand still!" Wentworth hissed suddenly. Clock ticks! They must be here somewhere, the ticking of the clock that was speeding them to their doom. He flung himself to his knees, bending his head to listen. Muffled, distant they came to him. Even as he listened there was a brief catch such as an alarm clock might make the instant before the alarm sounded. That click told that bomb would burst within heartbeats.

But Wentworth had found the bomb now.

With the consciousness of death in his heart, the hope that he still might save his country in his mind, he flung himself on a small metal trap door that opened into an oiling pit beneath the elevator machinery. The door yanked up, flew wide in the same gesture. Wentworth's hands scooped down into the pit, closed on an irregularly shaped object of steel to which a round-faced clock was affixed.

As he pulled the thing upward toward him, his eyes stared down at the white face of the clock. The hand almost touched the contact lever at twelve. Within a thought of time, that metal hand would touch that metal point and the current from those batteries would set off God alone knew what terrific burst of explosive.

Coiled wires ran from the clock, into the oval of steel that was the bomb. Wentworth's fingers seized those wires. He wrenched savagely with one hand. He balled the other into a fist, smashed the glass that covered the dial of the clock, striking so that his palm, breaking through, would smear the fatal hand away from that contact point that meant death—that meant the doom of the nation.

There was a thin clatter of breaking glass. Wentworth felt the bite of the sharp fragments into his palm. Never had he known a more grateful pain, for beneath his staring eyes he saw the black hand bend back from the contact. An instant later, the wires snapped loose, too. Wentworth knelt on the concrete floor and stared down at the bomb. He held his breath. With a whirring metallic snap the clock reached twelve, but there were no contact points to flash destruction into the tube that held the explosive. Wentworth blew out a long slow breath.

Carefully he removed every wire from the bomb. Not until then did he place the thing aside and reel to his feet. He didn't know that he was so weak. He turned and Nita ran into his arms with a little cry of gladness.

"I've won," Wentworth stammered crazily. "I've won! The leaders are dead or captured. It will be easy now to scatter the rest." He lifted his head and his eyes sought the upward heights. He thanked whatever providence there was that Nita's heels had sounded like clock ticks on the concrete floor of this cell that might have meant death.

A man's deep voice broke in upon his silent thanks. "I was not aware, *Señor* Wentworth," it said, "that you knew my daughter so well."

Wentworth looked across Nita's dear head pillowed on his

chest to see Don Estéban standing on the steps. Jackson was behind him.

"He wouldn't go, sir," Jackson reported. "I couldn't force him away in time to do any good, so we stayed. He wouldn't believe that his daughter wasn't his daughter."

Wentworth flung back his head and laughed. The sound was cracked and queer. Once more Jackson explained the trick that had been played by Nita and Wentworth—added his assurances that Carmencita was safe.

"I think you'll find that she's cured of her affection for Scott Haillie," he said dryly.

Don Estéban shook his head wearily. "I'm afraid you don't know the Janández women," he said. Despite his weariness there was a pride in his voice.

Wentworth nodded his head decisively. "She'll be cured of it," he said. "Because I think it very likely we'll find Haillie dead when we go upstairs."

"Dead!" It was a cry from three throats.

"I think," Wentworth went on, "that Haillie couldn't take his own medicine in the end—that he cut his own throat with that little ring-knife—rather than wait for the bomb to go off. I heard his screams for help stop some time ago—at least a minute."

Jackson snorted. He said then what he said later when they found that Wentworth's words were truth. He sneered and said:

"So you couldn't take it, Mr. Pirate?"